# A Merry Scary Christmas

## By Various Authors

Copyright ©2014 by Yvonne Mason

Published by Dressing your Book
www.dressingyourbook.com
Key Largo Florida

ISBN: 978-1-941912-27-0

# Table of Contents

Quota by Shawna Platt ........................................1

The Cross Examining by Chad Lutzke ....................39

The Hobo and the Laymen by Victor George Matak.....59

This Little Piggy by Sandy Rozanski ....................753

Christmas Dreams Come True by Tara Atkinson.......843

Three Elves by L. Vera ....................................890

Christmas Eve by Yvonne Mason ..........................92

The Bad Shelf Elf by G.J. Lentz........................104

Dirty Santa by Marvin Anderson ...................... 12929

Under the Mistletoe by Gianandrea Maoli .............131

Oranment by Rick Powell................................149

The Woman in the Upstairs Window by Chris Gonzales 171

Along the Way by Alan Gravitt..........................1811

Christmas Massacre by Sheri Ann Richerson ...........204

The Kingdom Art Murder by Ian Bush ..................216

Quota

By Shawna Platt

Shawna Platt known as Angel Shadow has published a poetry book, Wicked Winds, which became a bestseller and her self-help/personal growth book, Bridging the Gap: Healing the Shadows Within. She is currently writing her third book. She is a featured author on Peter Shepherd's Trans4mind website. Some of her articles are available via podcast. Podcast #'s: 11, 13, 17, 22, 33, 76, 77, 127, 155, 156, 157, 158 & 239. As a survivor, Angel Shadow dedicates much of her time to the awareness and prevention of child abuse and domestic violence. She is an article contributor on Yvonne Mason's domestic violence website. On March 18, 2010, she was the 60th guest on The Funky Writer Radio Show. Website:

http://guardianangel117.wix.com/authorangelshadow

# Quota
# By Shawna Platt

There it was, right on the front page of Cromwell Creek's local paper. The local serial killer had struck again and Rachel Cromwell was proud of her latest piece. She busted her butt to make sure she had her facts straight before writing this one. She looked up from the paper as her husband, Daryl, entered the kitchen.

"Check it out! My article made the front page!" she said as she handed it to him.

He glanced at the paper and read the headline. *Local Serial Killer Strikes Again!* He took a deep breath and placed it on the table.

She leaned against the counter. "Aren't you going to read it?"

"After breakfast."

She grabbed the coffee pot off the warmer and refilled her cup. "Want me to make you a plate?"

"No. I can get it." Daryl was in a grumpy mood and didn't feel like listening to his wife's rant about her recent assignment. He piled a plate with food, sat at the table, and shoved the paper aside. Rachel filled another cup and placed it in front of him.

"How can you be so calm about all this? We have a serial killer loose in our town and this is the fourth victim found in two weeks." She sat at the other side of the table and studied him. "Body parts missing." No response. "Body parts haven't been found." Still nothing. He simply sat and stuffed his mouth with food. "Apparently, you don't care that people are being slaughtered again. Year after year, it's the same thing." She rose and put her cup in the sink. "Why Christmas? Why does it always happen during the month of December?"

Daryl placed his fork on the table and wiped his mouth. "It's probably a pack of wolves. We have plenty of them here in Montana."

Katy Perry's Firework erupted from her cell phone before she could respond. "Hello? Yes! Yes, of course! I'll be right in." She pushed off the edge of the counter. "I have to go in to the office. The police found some new evidence last night and the editor wants to go over it with me."

Her husband stood with his plate and walked to the sink. After he rinsed it, he leaned in and kissed her cheek. "You go do what you do. I have a full day of appointments, so I may be late getting home tonight."

"Okay. Stay safe out there, especially after dark." She walked away, blasting the words of her current favorite song. ...*Baby, you're a firework. Come on; show 'em what you're worth*...

He shook his head, refilled his cup, and sat back down at the table. He extended his arm and pulled the paper to him. *Local Serial Killer Strikes Again!* He ran his fingers through his hair. What was happening to his town? Yes, his town. Cromwell Creek, Montana had been founded by his bloodline many generations ago, but most of the family abandoned their town and he resented them for it. Cromwell Creek wasn't good enough for them. Now, the Cromwell bloodline was scattered all over the US and he was left to keep the home fires burning, but no one ever came back for a visit.

Cromwell Creek wasn't exactly a small town, but not a big city, either. It was right in the middle. Not too big, not too small. Homey, without being podunkville, but not overrun with endless faces no one recognized. Daryl was one of the town's doctors, as his father was before him. He met Rachel when she stayed over in Cromwell Creek for a night, traveling for an assignment. She was a budding journalist from Seattle with big dreams, on her way to Chicago to cover a new museum opening. A co-worker told her about Cromwell Creek and said she should spend the night and enjoy the beautiful Montana scenery. She had dinner with Daryl that night and just happened to stay in Cromwell Creek again on her way back to Seattle. They made the long distance relationship work for almost a year, and then he decided to propose to her atop Seattle's Space Needle while visiting one weekend. Two months later, she packed up, moved to Montana, and got a job as a journalist for Cromwell Creek's newspaper. A year and a half later, Drake came along, and they'd been trying to live the family dream ever since.

Drake, now sixteen, wasn't your typical teenage boy. Over the years, he'd become quiet and withdrawn. He kept to himself most of the time, listening to music or watching television. Rachel and Daryl did their best to get him into the social scene, but Drake wasn't interested. The few friends he did have were always inviting him over, but Drake would rather spend his time locked up in his bedroom. School was difficult for him, socially and academically. He was always on the sidelines, watching and lurking. It's not that he was unattractive, quite the opposite was true. He had the attention of many teenage females to prove it. He dressed well, thanks to his dad's salary as a doctor, but something was just off about him, and no one could pull him out of his self-created prison. He was simply *born that way*, according to his mother. Rachel loved her son, but she was at the end of her rope.

Daryl finished reading Rachel's serial killer article, set the paper aside, and rested his face in his hands. *Not again*, he thought, *I can't go through this again*. It was less than a week before Christmas and he wanted this year to be different. Reality was closing in on him and he wished it would stop. Why couldn't Rachel just leave it alone? One way or another, he had to protect Drake. He pushed away from the table, grabbed his keys, and headed for the front door. He stopped for a moment to look at their Christmas tree. He loved what the tree represented, but wished he could celebrate it on an emotional level. This year would be like all the others the past few years. *It shouldn't be this way. Not at Christmas*. He took one last look at the tree and headed out the door.

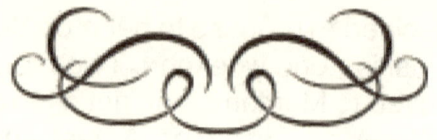

Rachel sat, frozen, at her desk. She couldn't believe what was in front of her eyes. The police had dropped off a photograph of a slightly bloody shoe they found at the crime scene the night before. She pulled the photograph closer and inspected it. There was no denying it. It was Drake's shoe, or one that looked just like it. She would check his closet when she returned home and see if one was missing. Brad Lamont, her editor and boss, stood beside her desk.

"What do you think?"

"I think it's a shoe. What does it look like?"

"Hey, don't get defensive with me. I know it's a shoe, but whose shoe? Victim or killer?"

Rachel looked at the photo again and shrugged. "I don't know."

"I don't expect you to know, but I do expect you to try and find out. You wanted this assignment."

"I've had this assignment for years now, Brad. What makes you think this year will be any different? Whoever's responsible for the murders continues to elude us all."

"Just do your best. Maybe this year will be the turning point." He turned and left her office. *He's such an ass*, she thought; *no wonder he's still single.*

She looked at the photo again and thought to herself, *Yeah, this year could be the turning point, all right.* She sat back in her chair and listened to the silence around her. It was too quiet. Why did it always have to be so quiet?

Drake sat at his desk and leaned on his elbow with his hand on the side of his face. He hated school, and pretty much, everyone in it. He gazed out the window and wished for freedom. His life was a joke. He got along well with his dad, but his mom was pushy and demanding. Nothing was ever good enough for her. He'd show her someday. She thought he didn't know, but he did. He knew, all right, and she'd pay for it. *Yeah*, he thought, *maybe this would be the year she'd pay for it.* The bell ending class snapped him to and he loaded his books in his arms and filed his way to the hall with the rest of the cattle. At least today was the last day before Christmas vacation.

Lunch was uneventful, as usual. He sat in the corner and watched the fake exchange of emotions take place. *People are strange animals*, he thought. He opened his notebook and scribbled. He looked up again and smiled. More like a sneer. Should he warn them? He never had before, but maybe this would put some excitement back in the game.

Rachel rushed through the front door and marched straight up the stairs to Drake's room. She opened his closet door and started digging. Every shoe had a mate, and the shoe missing a mate, the one in question, could not be found. She sat on the floor and dug deeper. There it was, tucked in the back corner, the other shoe from the photo with traces of blood. She sat back and stared at the evidence in front of her. What was she going to do with this? She pushed off the floor, went to her bedroom, and opened her walk-in closet. She found an old luggage bag and stuffed the shoe inside. She grabbed some sweaters off their hangers and stuffed them in as well. She placed the luggage bag on the top corner shelf and stacked other bags on top of it. She sat on the edge of her bed and listened. Why did it always have to be so quiet?

Daryl sat on the park bench outside his office building. It was cold, too cold to be sitting on a park bench, but he didn't care. It was snowing again; it always snowed in Montana in December and it was one of the things he loved about it. He thought about Rachel and her obsession. She thought he didn't know, but he did, and she had to be stopped. There was only one way out of this and Drake had to be kept safe. This year, her obsession would stop. He'd make sure of it. He glanced at his watch and realized his next patient would be coming soon. He rose from the bench and walked toward his office building, feeling the shadow following close behind, and had a plan formulating in his mind on how he could stop Rachel from doing more harm.

Rachel sat on the couch and took another sip of wine. Daryl would be home soon and she had to find a way to talk to him about Drake. What was she going to do with the shoe evidence? Should she continue to hide it and wait for the best time to bring it forward? When *was* the best time? She had to plan it out carefully. For years, she'd been hiding the secret and now it was getting out of hand. She leaned back on the couch and swirled the wine in her glass. Everything was about to blow up in her face. How she hated Montana and the life she'd built here. She wished she'd stayed in Seattle instead of moving to this god-forsaken town. The last few years had been building up to this moment and she wasn't about to have it ruined now. *Stay calm*, she told herself. *You can do this.* Family or not, she had to finish it.

She was still seated on the couch, on her third glass of wine, when Daryl returned from work. The alcohol she'd consumed had built up the courage she needed to address the issue. She held her glass up, as in a toast, and smiled when he walked in the room. "We have to talk about Drake."

Daryl stood for a moment, accessing the situation. He sighed deeply and sat on the couch next to her. He watched as she swirled her wine, hating the person she'd become. "What do you want to talk about?"

"Drake, of course."

"Yes, you said that. What about Drake?"

She tried to sit forward, but gravity was no longer cooperating. He pulled her by the arm to a full sitting position, took her wine, and set it on the coffee table. She pointed a not so steady finger in his direction.

"Drake is in trouble."

"Drake is fine."

She shook her head. "No! No, he isn't. He's got some serious problems that need to be addressed." She paused. "I found the shoe."

His brow creased at her words. "What shoe?"

She swayed on the couch. "His other shoe. The missing mate. Bloody. I have it, you know. This missing shoe."

He moved in closer. "What are you planning to do with this....shoe?"

She swayed again and fell against the back of the couch. "I don't know yet, but I have a plan." She pointed her finger at him again. "A really good plan." She laughed.

He stood and held a hand out to her. "You're drunk and need to go to bed. You have no idea what you're talking about. Drake is not in trouble and I have no idea what you're talking about regarding the shoe."

"They found a shoe at the crime scene. It matches Drake's, but I could only find one, and it's bloody. What do you think that means?"

He grabbed her by the arm and jerked her off the couch. "It means you're drunk. Are you accusing your own son of murder?"

She wobbled in front of him, and when she spoke, her breath smelled like a stale wine barrel. "I don't know what to think anymore." She pushed away and made her way upstairs. It took a few tries, and Daryl thought she'd fall back down them, but after a moment, he heard the bedroom door close. He ran his fingers through his hair. He had to speak to Drake about the shoe. What had Rachel done? Whatever it was, this time she went too far.

The following evening was Friday night and the town of Cromwell Creek had their annual Christmas caroling event. Members of the community would get together and walk around town singing carols. Downtown had a small square in the middle of it, with trees, park benches, and a gazebo. There was a small fountain, filled with coins, but the water was frozen. Ice cascaded down the tri-level fountain, forming beautiful icicles. The town square was the location of many town gatherings and tonight was no exception. The town council had a large Christmas tree set up in the middle of the square, festive and full of lights. Everyone was here, dressed for the weather, and ready to have some fun. Rachel sat on one of the benches and watched the people come and go. She resented their holiday glee. *What fools*, she thought. *How could anyone be happy in Cromwell Creek? What a wasted life.* She kept a close eye on Daryl and Drake, careful not to let them out of her sight. She tried to recall the night before. Had she talked to Daryl about Drake and the shoe? She couldn't remember, and Daryl didn't mention it this morning. Wouldn't he have mentioned it? It was a big deal and she figured he'd bring it up and want to discuss it. Or would he? She knew the secret, even if he didn't realize it, and the secret would come out soon.

She noticed Cromwell Creek's homeless man. That's what the town called him. Not by his name, Stan, he was just *the homeless man*. She rolled her eyes at him. *What a waste!*

Brad walked up to Rachel and sat beside her. "You should be covering this event. Why are you just sitting here?"

"Do I have to work twenty-four-seven? Can't you see I'm enjoying the festivities?"

He laughed. "Oh, yes! You look like you're having a grand time."

She leaned forward and pinched the bridge of her nose with two fingers. "I have a headache and I'm not in the mood."

"Sorry to hear that, but I expect a piece on the evening's festivities for tomorrow's paper."

"Why can't someone else do it?"

"Are you kidding? And let you miss out on the big stuff? Not a chance. You wanted this job and you're the best I've got. You want to keep making the big bucks; you'll have a piece ready in the morning." He patted her on the shoulder and walked away.

She sneered at him as he approached a couple by the tree. "Yeah, big bucks, my ass! I should have stayed in Seattle." She glanced over to Daryl and Drake's location. They were nowhere to be found. She stood and looked around the square. No sight of them anywhere. She hated Brad even more for distracting her. She walked across the street to the local diner and peered through the window. The hustle and bustle inside made it impossible to see. She thought she caught the back of Drake's head, but someone moved in front of her line of vision. *Where did they go?* She had to keep an eye on their every move until her plan was complete. Doing this would be next to impossible, as her job took up much of her time. She couldn't follow Daryl to work or be with Drake every waking moment. She'd have to kick things up a notch. It was time to get the ball rolling and finish this once and for all. She looked around to make sure she hadn't drawn attention to herself and slipped into the back alley behind the diner. She leaned against the building and took a deep breath. Even with all the noise from the festivities, it was too quiet. Why was it always so quiet? The shadow always accompanied the quiet and it had followed her. No physical body could be seen to cast the shadow, but the shadow was there nonetheless.

The next morning, Daryl stood in front of the television, remote in hand, and shook his head. The local morning news was covering the newest victim of Cromwell Creek's serial killer. His fuzzy head heard the report in chunks: a high school student, a senior, a football player from a prominent family, body pieces missing, found in the alley behind the diner. Drake stood behind the couch. When Daryl heard Rachel coming down the stairs, he turned off the television. He exchanged a knowing glance with Drake, who nodded and quickly left the room.

Rachel shot into the room like a rocket, pulling her coat on. "There's been another murder. A high school boy."

"I know."

She simply glanced at him. "You know? That's all you're going to say?"

"What else would you like me to say, Rachel?"

"Don't you care at all?"

Daryl laughed. "Yes, Rachel, I care."

"This is going to end soon. I'll make sure of it. I'll tie this all together with a nice little bow for the police. I'm getting close."

"I'm happy for you. You better do it soon."

She turned to leave, but spun around. "Did I talk to you last night about the shoe?"

He looked confused. "No. What shoe?"

She stared at him for a moment with narrow eyes. "Nothing. Never mind." She turned and stormed out the door. He walked to the window and watched her back out of the driveway.

"No, Rachel. You won't be figuring anything out. After I'm done with you, you won't be doing much of anything."

He turned, walked up the stairs to their bedroom, and opened the closet. He only had to look a moment. He pulled the luggage bags off the top corner shelf and took the large one from the bottom of the pile. He opened it and shook out the contents. There it was the missing shoe. He placed the sweaters back in the bag and put them all back on the top shelf, then went downstairs and got a small garbage bag from under the sink. He placed the shoe inside and went to the garden shed. He loosened a number of boards on the floor until the dirt below was exposed, placed the garbage bag in the hole, and covered it. He replaced the boards, made sure they were secure, and moved the lawn mower over the spot. He wiped his hand across his brow. *No, Rachel. I don't think you'll be doing much of anything,* he thought. He returned to the house and cleaned up. It was Saturday and he had a few hours of free time to work on his plan. He sat at the table and picked up his phone. The shadow sat in the chair beside him, a smile on his face.

Rachel sat at her desk looking over her file on the Cromwell family. For years, she'd collected information on Daryl's family history, and what a history they had. No wonder all the normal people who happened to have the Cromwell name fled this place. Daryl's father, Victor Cromwell, had been suspected of cannibalism. According to some, he had a quota. Every year, a certain number had to be sacrificed, portions of their bodies eaten. It was never proven, so he walked away, but she knew the secret. Daryl was a cannibal and now he was preparing her son to continue the family legacy. She knew Drake was too far gone for her to reach, so she'd have to take him down, too. The shoe was her smoking gun, and when the time was right, she'd present it to the authorities. She'd be free from this bullshit town and move back to Seattle.

*Why don't you just leave?* She tried to push the voice away. *You're crazy, Rachel. Loony balloony. That's what they'll call you!*

"I'm not crazy!" She stood and paced her office. "Why is it so quiet?"

*You can't stop the silence. It's the only way you can hear me.*

"I can stop the silence! You never existed until the silence of this place took over. Once I'm back in Seattle, you'll go away!"

*You're talking to yourself again, Rachel, and you're wrong. You don't know how wrong you are.*

She sat back down at her desk and found her favorite song on her phone… *Baby, you're a firework*… and drowned out the voice. Lately, this song was the only thing that kept her sane.

Daryl and Drake sat at the local diner having lunch. Daryl shook his fork at his son.

"You need to start doing better in school."

Drake bit into his hamburger and spoke through a mouthful of food. "Why? I don't see any point in it."

"You need to finish school. It's not an option, son."

Drake shrugged and sucked soda through a straw. "I know. Doesn't mean I have to like it." He sat back and twirled his straw in the glass. "What are we going to do about mom? She's losing it!"

Daryl wiped his mouth with a napkin and sighed. "I know. Every year it gets worse."

"She isn't aware that we know, right?"

"No. She still thinks she's getting away with setting us up."

"What are you going to do?"

Daryl leaned forward and ruffled his son's hair. "I'll handle your mom, don't you worry about it."

Drake smiled. He trusted his dad more than anyone. "Don't let her ruin your plans."

"I have no intention of letting that happen. I made some more calls this morning."

"I still can't believe she'd do this to her husband and son. What kind of monster is she?"

"I don't think she knows what she's doing anymore."

"It's kind of sad, really."

Daryl nodded. "Yes, it is." He motioned to Drake to grab his coat. "Let's go. I have some stuff to work on at home."

"So, you sure you're going to be all right?"

Daryl patted his son on the shoulder. "Yes, son. We're both going to be fine. I promise."

"Can you drop me off at Jeff's?"

"Yes! Of course! I'm happy to see you socializing a bit more."

"It's Saturday, why not? I don't have anything else to do and I'd rather not be around mom."

"She went into the office today and I'll be home for most of it, but I do have some errands to run later."

"Okay. I'll be home later tonight."

Drake returned home before his dad that night and found his mom on the couch, with her beloved glass of wine. He sighed and tried to go undetected to his room. Her voice called out before he made it to the stairs.

"Drake? Is that you? We need to talk."

He blew out a breath and walked back to the living room. "You bellowed."

She shook the wine glass in front of her. "Don't take that tone with me. I have a question."

He stood a moment, waiting. "And your question is?"

She tried to stand and had to use the couch for support. "Why are you missing a shoe?"

He gave her a confused look. "What shoe? What are you talking about?"

"You're missing a shoe. It doesn't have its bloody mate. Like to explain?"

He took a step back. "I don't know, Mom. Where is the shoe?"

"Oh, I know where both shoes are, young man. Don't think you can fool me."

"Well, if you know where both shoes are, I'm not missing a shoe, am I?" He turned and rushed up the stairs. She was really starting to scare him.

Rachel fell back on the couch and spilled most of her wine. She yelled in the direction of the stairs. "See what you made me do, people eater? I know the secret!" She closed her eyes and tried to stop the spinning. She put her palm across her forehead and took a deep breath. *I can't believe Daryl is grooming my son*, she thought. *Just like his dad did with him.* She leaned forward on her knees. How could she have been so stupid? She should have returned to Seattle years ago, but the silence took over, the voices started, and the shadow followed her everywhere. She'd reached her breaking point. This had to end and then she could escape. She rose from the couch and walked to the window. It was snowing. *Of course, it's snowing!* She looked out on the blanket of white, silent and menacing. Why did it have to be so quiet? And there it was, the shadow casting its dark body across the white snow. *Just leave me alone, you bastard!* She walked to the end of the window and closed the blinds.

Drake stood in front of the grave marker. It was 2am and he came here when he couldn't sleep. He knelt in front of his grandfather's grave. "It's all falling apart. You're dying wish, and it's falling apart. She has to be stopped."

He detected the shadow out of the corner of his eye, but when he turned nothing was there. He took the sleeve of his coat and brushed the accumulated dirt and dust off the tombstone. "I'm sorry, Grandpa! We're trying." The shadow moved again to the other side of him. He glanced in the direction of the movement and noticed what looked like a fresh grave being dug. He walked over to get a closer look and found a fresh hole in the ground, a mound of dirt piled beside it. He assumed this grave was being prepared for the high school boy recently killed. He shook his head and walked back to his grandfather's grave. "We really are trying." He hung his head, turned, and walked through the graveyard, fully aware of the shadow's eyes on him.

The shadowed figure watched him pass. Watched him as he weaved through the headstones. Drake would stop once in a while and look, then move on to the next one. The shadow followed him through the graveyard. Drake stopped and listened. The graveyard remained quiet for a few moments and then …*snap*… a twig broke to his right. He spun to see an old man walking toward a grave close by. He recognized Stan, the homeless man. He'd always felt sorry for the old guy. Drake walked toward him and held out his hand.

"Hi. I'm Drake."

The old man stared at the grave. "I know who you are."

Drake stepped next to the old man and tried to make small talk even though he knew the answer to the question. "Someone you know?"

The old man nodded. "My wife. I lost everything when I lost her."

Drake read the tombstone: *My Beloved Wife*. The line below that: *Evelyn*. He sighed. "Look, you really shouldn't be out here tonight. Let me walk you back to town."

The man shook his head. "I'll stay here as long as I please. You can't make me go."

"No, I can't, but I think you should head back to town now."

The man turned and snarled, exposing rotten teeth. "I'll stay as long as I please! Go away!"

Drake took a step back. "Fine, old man, have it your way. I warned you."

Drake turned to leave and the old man grabbed him by the sleeve, leaned into him, and thrust his foul smelling breath in his face. Drake was surprised at his physical strength. "Don't think I don't know! I've lived here a long time. I know lots of things!"

Drake pulled his sleeve from the man's grasp. "You don't know shit, old man."

"You Cromwell's think you're so smart. Better than everyone else. Ran you all out years ago, but your father thinks he's so smart. No one listens to the old homeless man, but I know! I know plenty!" A tear rolled down his cheek. "Don't think I don't know what happened to my wife. The police wouldn't listen, but I'll show them."

"Just what are you going to show them? You've got nothing."

"I've got plenty. Just you wait and see! They'll listen to me soon enough. I've got lots to show them."

Drake took two steps back. "Careful, old man. You don't know what you're messing with."

"I told you, I know plenty. Get away from me!"

Drake turned and walked back to his grandfather's grave. "Falling apart. It's all falling apart!"

The shadow remained hidden.

Rachel woke at 5am to the sound of voices coming from Drake's room. She rolled over to find the spot next to her in bed empty. She rose from the bed and quietly walked to Drake's door. Daryl was inside and she could hear them talking.

"She doesn't think I know, Dad. How long will this continue?"

"For now, just avoid your mom."

"How did she find out and why is she doing this?"

"Well, she is a journalist, son. It's what she does. Why she would want to check out the history of my family, I don't know."

"But she's losing it. I swear she's gone crazy with it all. And what about Grandpa's dying wish? She's ruining everything."

"I agree she needs to be stopped and I'm working on a plan. Just hang in there a little bit longer."

"I talked to the homeless guy when I visited grandpa's grave this morning."

"I told you to quit going to the graveyard in the middle of the night."

"I know, sorry. I couldn't sleep. Anyway, he was there again, but this time I talked to him. I swear he's crazy, too!"

"He has his demons like the rest of us and some demons are impossible to escape from."

"Maybe he'd be better off if he went to be with his wife," Drake said with a grin.

"That may be true." Daryl ruffled his son's hair. "How much sleep did you get last night?"

"Enough, I guess."

"It's Sunday. Get some more."

"Sounds good to me. Talk to you later, Dad."

Rachel stumbled trying to get away from the door. From inside Drake's room, Daryl put his finger to his lips and Drake froze. She rushed down the hall to her bedroom and closed the door. She fell on the bed and took a deep breath. *They know? What do they think they know?* She had to get out of this house, this insanely quiet house.

Daryl opened Drake's door and found the hallway empty. He turned back to Drake. "Get some more sleep. We'll talk later."

"Dad?"

"Yes, Son?"

"Christmas is in two days."

Daryl nodded.

"There has to be one more by Christmas or the quota won't be met."

"I know, Son, I know. I'll take care of it."

Rachel left the house without speaking to Daryl. She drove into town and sat in the local diner, sipping coffee. *What do they know?* She looked out the window and saw the homeless man walking around the town square. She didn't understand why he was homeless. From what she was told, he was a lifelong resident of Cromwell Creek, so why did everyone let him wander around? She'd have to dig into his story next.

She leaned her head back against the booth. *My husband's a cannibal.* She couldn't believe she was admitting it. *Not only is my husband a cannibal, he's making my son one, too.* She leaned forward and put her head in her hands. Tomorrow night was Christmas Eve and the quota had to be met. According to her calculations, there had to be one more victim. She had to act fast. A loud tap on the window made her jump. She looked up to see the homeless man standing there. He pointed his finger toward his chest, and mouthed the words, *I know.* She fled the booth and ran outside. He was easy to catch up to as he made his way down the sidewalk. She raced in front of him and stopped him in his tracks.

"You know what?"

He simply stared at her.

"What do you know? Don't play games with me."

"I know everything. It was supposed to stop with my Evelyn. I lost everything when I lost her."

"I don't know what you're talking about. Explain."

"You have it all right in front of you. You *know*. What are you going to do about it?"

She shook her head as the silence surrounded her. She saw the shadow sleek around the corner and stand there. If it had eyes, it would have been staring at them.

"Fine. Suit yourself. They'll listen to me soon enough." He shuffled off and around the corner, out of sight. The shadow remained in front of her, tilted what looked like its head, and folded back around the corner.

She went back inside the diner and paid her bill. *They'll listen to him? What does he know? Everyone thinks they know!* Homeless man Stan wasn't going to talk to anyone. He wasn't ruining this for her. She'd planned too carefully for some homeless guy to come along and screw it up. They would definitely be meeting again.

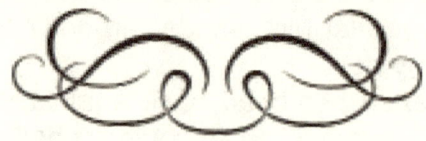

There he was, standing in front of her grave again. He could always be found in front of her grave at this early hour of the morning, in his ratty old coat. *You're too predictable, Stan.* The figure dressed in black approached quietly. Without turning around, Stan spoke.

"I know you're there." He turned to face the figure cloaked in black. He couldn't make out the face, but he knew there was one under the hood. A ski mask, perhaps? This wasn't like the shadow that followed him around. No, this was an actual person. "What do you want? I ain't hurtin' no one."

"You've done enough damage."

Stan cocked his head. The voice sounded familiar, but he couldn't place it. It was deep, almost like a growl. He shook his head and turned back to his wife's grave. The figure pulled a large serrated hunting knife out from under their cloak. Stan could feel the danger from behind, but he didn't care. The first hit to the side of his neck took him to his knees. He instinctively put his hand over the wound and cried out in pain. The second hit from the knife hit his spine at the base of his neck and he felt his body go numb. The last thing he remembered was seeing his wife's name coming at him as he fell against her tombstone.

The cloaked figure used the serrated edge of the knife to remove Stan's head from his body. Then tossed it on Evelyn's grave and pulled the body to Victor Cromwell's grave. The knife cut into flesh as they removed both arms and legs and tossed them on Victor's grave. He placed the torso in a large black garbage bag and swung it over their shoulder. He would put this bag with the rest of the extra body parts. "No one will ever find the rest of you, Stan. They never find the rest of the bodies. I make sure of that." He wiped the splatter from his face with a gloved hand and looked around. "So much blood. You were a messy one, Stan the Man." He walked over to Evelyn's grave and positioned Stan's head so it was looking out. "There, now you can see the world." He turned and walked away, bagged torso over his shoulder, whistling a quiet tune. The shadow watched from a distance.

Daryl rolled over and stared at the ceiling. It was 5 am on Christmas Eve morning. He knew today would be life changing. This year so many things had gone wrong. The whole game changed when he realized his wife was involved and he didn't know how to stop it. One way or another, he would end it by tonight. He heard Rachel in the shower and wondered why she was up so early. He reached over to the table beside the bed and grabbed the remote to turn on the television. The local morning news was on. *Of course,* he thought, *what else would Rachel watch? Every TV in the house would be set on the news if she had her way.* This morning, however, what he saw made him bolt upright in bed. Stan's picture was shown in the corner of the screen, while the newscaster told of his violent murder the night before; parts of his body found on the graves of his wife and Victor Cromwell. Rachel walked out of the bathroom, wrapped in her robe. He shot her a sideways glance and pointed to the TV.

"What the hell? Stan? Why would anyone want to hurt Stan?"

She sat on the edge of the bed and watched the rest of the report. She rose slowly and looked at her husband. "What's going on, Daryl?"

"I don't know, Rachel, why don't you tell me."

She turned and grabbed her phone, dialed Brad's number. He didn't even say hello. "I was just getting ready to call you. Get in here now! We're in serious crisis mode!" and hung up.

"Shit!" She tossed her phone on the bed and rushed to the closet. She threw on the first thing she found that somewhat matched and raced toward the door. Daryl sat, frozen on the bed, as the newscaster hit the highlights of the story again. He shook his head.

"The quota has been met for another year."

Rachel and Brad ducked under the crime scene tape and entered the small section of cemetery covered in blood. From Evelyn's grave to Victor Cromwell's, it was nothing but a red stain. Tombstones were splattered. Concrete angel faces were covered in red. Flowers left behind by loved ones, now became part of a horror story. Brad covered his mouth for a moment.

"There has never been this much blood before. What the hell happened?"

Rachel stepped forward and noticed a small blanket covering something on Evelyn's grave. She walked to it and reached for it. A police officer reached down and grabbed her arm.

"I wouldn't do that if I were you."

She pulled away from his grasp. "Good thing I'm not you." She jerked the blanket away and saw Stan's lifeless eyes staring back. She jumped back. "Holy shit!" She threw the blanket back over the severed head and tried to stand. The officer sighed.

"Sorry, I tried to warn you."

"I've never seen anything like this. This is the worst of all crime scenes so far." She looked at the officer. "What kind of evidence have you found?"

"So far, we've found nothing but Stan's blood."

"Nothing? You've found nothing? No trace evidence at all? A hair, piece of clothing?"

He shook his head. "Once again, whoever did this was clean. Nothing but the victim's blood and what body parts they decided to leave behind."

"This is crazy! There has to be something!" She glanced at the blanket covering Stan's head. "Do you realize that blanket alone could have compromised evidence?" She shook her head and walked back to Brad, waited while he finished talking to one of the officers. "Well?"

Brad looked around at the blood bath. "They've got nothing, as usual."

"That's unacceptable! How can there be nothing here?"

Brad rubbed his hands in circles over his cheeks. "We have to solve this, Rachel."

She laughed. "We're not the police, Brad, but if things keep going the way they are, we'll solve this before they do."

Brad nodded and handed her his 35mm camera. "You brought your own car. Take this and get as many shots as you can. All angles. If the police object, tell them you'll share the photos you take. We have to do our part and work together with the officials on this." He walked back toward his car.

"And where do you think you're going?" she yelled at his back.

He turned and walked backward. "Back to the office. I have some research to do. Meet me there when you have the photos, we'll download them and take a good look."

She lifted the camera, focused, and began taking pictures. None of the officers seemed to object. The close ups were the most difficult and Evelyn's grave made her stomach turn. Stan's head, leaned against the tombstone, cold dead eyes staring; his mouth wide open, as if froze in mid scream; his rotten teeth exposed. She expected bugs and worms to come crawling out any second. She got a few more shots and had to turn away. An officer walked up to her.

"You all right, Rachel?"

She nodded and took a deep breath. "Yes, I'm fine, thank you." She blew out another hard breath. "This is a bad one."

The officer looked around. "The worst we've seen, mess wise. Normally, we just find a body with parts missing. Blood is always localized to the area of the body." He took off his police cap and rubbed his head. "This..." he waved a hand, "I'm just speechless."

Rachel raised the camera again and got a full shot of the area. "Whoever it is, they were pissed off at the homeless guy."

"Stan. His name was Stan."

"Of course, I'm sorry."

"And, yeah, pissed off. I wonder who'll be next?" He walked away before she could answer.

She quietly replied, "There won't be a *next*. The quota has been met." She took a few more photos and headed back to her car. A group had formed at the crime scene tape and they shot questions to her as she got into her car.

"Is it true? Is it really Stan?"

"What can you tell us, Rachel?"

"Why would someone do this?"

"Why can't you authority people figure this out?"

She shook her head and closed the door of her car. "Stinking rotten town. I can't wait to get out of here." In spite of all the noise outside, the silence took over, and the shadow watched from the blood-bathed scene.

Daryl and Drake sat on the couch in their living room. Drake, with a concerned look on his face, asked, "What about the shoe?"

"That's been taken care of. She can't use it."

"She won't stop. I swear she's going crazy."

"I know and I have a plan. This is what we're going to do." He picked up the phone and made a call.

Rachel sat at her desk and downloaded the photos from the crime scene. She knew the final pieces to the puzzle were now placed and she had to tie up the loose ends. The quota had been met for another year. It was time for all this to be over so she could escape, leaving her husband and son to deal with the aftermath. She'd finished writing up her piece on Stan's murder earlier and submitted it to Brad. He walked in as she finished loading the last few photos. "Just in time," she said, "I'm getting ready to take a closer look at the photos."

"Good. Maybe we'll find something the police missed."

"I doubt it, but let's take a look."

They spent the next hour going over the photos and found nothing new. Brad sat back and sighed. "Print these out. I want to take them home tonight and look them over again."

"There are over a hundred photos here."

"I don't care. Print them." He stood and stretched his back. "It's almost four o'clock and it's Christmas Eve. Print the photos and let's get out of here and enjoy our holiday."

"All right." She hit some buttons on her computer and started the printing process. "This will take some time."

"That's fine. I have some things I need to finish in my office. Let me know when they're ready."

By the time the photos printed and they'd finished their work, almost an hour had passed. She put the photos in a large envelope for Brad and took them to his office. He was putting on his coat as she walked in.

"Perfect timing. I was just coming to see if they were done printing yet."

"Yep. All there." She handed him the envelope. "What are your plans for the night?"

"As you know no wife and kids, so just a quiet night at home."

"But it's Christmas Eve. Aren't you lonely spending the holidays alone every year?"

He laughed. "No. If I wanted it to be different, I'd do something about it. My job is my wife and she takes up most of my time."

"If you're happy, that's all that matters." *Truth be told, I envy you.*

"Yes, I'm happy with my life the way it is."

"All right, Merry Christmas. I'll see you in a couple days." *Not if I have anything to say about it.*

"You, too. Tell Daryl and Drake Merry Christmas from me."

"Will do."

When she arrived home, the house appeared empty. "Hello?" No answer. Where were they? She checked upstairs. No one. She figured she might as well take advantage of whatever time she had. She went to her closet and pulled down the luggage bag. She opened it and removed the sweaters. The shoe was gone. She tore through the sweaters again. Nothing. She dumped the bag upside down, shook it. The shoe was gone. She sat on the floor and took a deep breath. *Breathe, Rachel. Just breathe. There's a logical explanation.* Her mind raced. One of them had the shoe. That's what they were talking about that morning in Drake's room. She was beyond paranoid and needed some wine. Yes, wine always helped calm her down. She went downstairs and filled her first glass. Where were Daryl and Drake and what were they up to?

After two glasses of wine, and many laps around the living room, she collapsed on the couch and tried to call them both again. No answer. Christmas Eve and they were probably out enjoying their little feast on Mr. Homeless Guy. *Oh, sorry. Stan. His name was Stan.* She pushed off the couch and stood in front of the window, watching the endless snowfall. How she hated Montana. She saw the shadow move across the white lawn and snarled at it. "You don't scare me anymore, you piece of shit. Whoever you are, whatever you are, I'm done with you and everything to do with this shit state." She closed the blinds as the shadow moved closer.

Rachel woke at 7 pm to her cell phone ringing. She grabbed it like a drowning victim to a life vest, looked at the display. It was Daryl. "Where the hell are you?"

"I don't have time, Rachel. Drake is in trouble and you need to come now."

"What do you mean he's in trouble? Where are you?"

"The abandoned warehouse. He's on the roof, threatening to jump. Come alone. No police. We'll handle this on our own."

"Did you take the shoe?"

"The shoe? Seriously? All you care about is the shoe? Yes, I have the fucking shoe. Get your ass here now!" He hung up.

"Son of a bitch!" She raced to the kitchen and grabbed the biggest knife she could find, wrapped it in a towel, and tucked it in her bag.

Rachel pulled up to the warehouse and parked beside Daryl's car. She looked to the roof, but it was too dark to see anything. She searched her glove compartment and found her emergency flashlight. She shined it in front of her. The small beam wouldn't do her much good. "Daryl? Where are you?" she called out.

She heard his voice echo from the back of the building. "Back here."

She pointed the flashlight in the direction of his voice and started walking. As she rounded the corner of the building, she called out again. "Daryl?"

"Up here." She saw a beam of light coming from a window, the glass broke out. "Find the door and use the stairs. Come to the third floor."

She shined her light around the side of the building until she found the broken door. She pushed through it and headed up the stairs. When she reached the third floor, she stayed by the stairs, and kept her distance from Daryl. He reached over, flipped a switch on a generator, and a portion of the third floor lit up. She moved to the side and remained in the shadows.

"Where is the shoe?"

"You and the god-damn shoe! That truly is all you care about!"

"I know your family's secret, Daryl. You may have got your hooks into Drake, but you're not taking me down with you."

"Apparently, you don't know as much as you think you do, Rachel."

"Your father was a cannibal. *You* are a cannibal and now you're grooming Drake, so the next generation is ready."

"Yes, my father was suspected of cannibalism, but it was never proven." He took a step closer to Rachel. "You think I'm the killer?"

"Don't play games with me, Daryl. Where is Drake? You said he was in trouble."

Daryl pointed to a corner of the third floor and she saw Drake's shadow sitting on a wooden crate.

"I'm right here, but you need to stay away from me."

Daryl took another step closer and raised his voice. "Answer me, Rachel! You think I'm the killer?"

"Of course, you're the killer. Look what you've got your son involved in. The police have the shoe from the crime scene; it's only a matter of time before they figure it out."

Daryl and Drake exchanged looks and Daryl dropped his chin to his chest. "I'm not the killer, Rachel, and neither is Drake. We were convinced it was you."

"You both truly are insane! Me? The killer?" She took a step toward the stairs. "You seriously don't think I'm going to believe you, do you? Trying to convince me you're not following in your father's footsteps. Nice try." She turned to flee down the stairs and was struck in the head with a pipe. She stumbled back and fell to the floor.

Brad stepped from the shadows, laughing. "Oh, look at all of you. You made it so easy." He pulled a gun from his coat and pointed it at Rachel, who was trying to stand. "You were so good. All those stories, making me shine. I just got to sit back and bask in the glory of my work. I really enjoyed those photos from the crime scene. You did me proud."

Rachel regained her footing and held her hand to the bloody wound on her forehead. "You're the killer?"

Brad took a step closer. "Had to have something to do to keep me from going stir crazy in this boring town. You know, you shouldn't leave research files on your desk. Victor Cromwell was quite an interesting read. All these years, so much fun."

Daryl positioned himself between Rachel and Brad, motioned to Drake. "Come and get your mom." Drake rushed over and helped his mom back to the wooden crate.

Daryl took a cautious step toward Brad. "Give me the gun."

Brad laughed. "Yeah, sure! Why don't I do that!" He waved the gun in the direction of Rachel and Drake. "I think I'll take care of them first." He then turned the gun to Daryl. "You and I will have some fun after that."

"You son of a bitch! All the innocent people you've killed over the last few years. And Stan," he paused, "I promised my father on his death bed I'd take care of Stan."

Brad leaned against a wooden pole. "Yeah, funny thing, huh? After what your father did to his poor wife, you're left with the burden of caring for him. You know, he didn't even fight me. It's like he wanted it. I did the poor bastard a favor."

"I tried to take care of him. He wouldn't let anyone close to him after that."

"Can't say I blame him. Like he'd want you taking care of him when your father was the one responsible for taking his whole life from him. Nope, he hated everyone after that."

Rachel spoke from the wooden crate she was seated on. "Daryl, why didn't you share all this with me?"

"What was I supposed to say, Rachel? Stan didn't want my help; he made that clear. I just wanted to forget it all. It happened long before I met you. I was still a teenager." He paused and took a step toward her. "I'm surprised people in town didn't tell you."

"No one told me anything. I've been driving myself crazy the past few years thinking you and Drake...." she trailed off, tried to shake the dizzy fog from her head. "All of this because I decided to do research on the Cromwell family and the foundation of this town."

Drake held the sleeve of his coat on his mother's wound. "I'm sorry, Mom. I'm sorry I thought you were the killer."

"I'm sorry, too, honey," she whispered.

Brad continued to lean against the pole, enjoying the scene unfolding before him.

Rachel looked at Daryl. "What was the issue with the shoe? It's been driving me crazy."

Brad sighed. "You all underestimate me, and since you'll all be dead soon, allow me to explain. I was covering a story on Cromwell Creek's high school sports. I was in the locker room when, your clumsy son here, came rushing in. Apparently, he cut his leg on something in the gym and the blood was running down all over his shoe. He took them off so his teacher could look at it, and was escorted to the nurse's station, leaving his shoes behind. I smeared some blood on the clean one by mistake when I was checking them out. The blood excited me. When I heard someone returning, I simply dropped one on my way out, didn't want to take the time to pick it up."

Rachel half laughed at Drake. "All this from a cut on your leg? Why didn't you tell me when I asked about the shoe?"

"You're hard enough on me as it is, so I didn't want you to know. When I came back to the locker room there was only one shoe. I wondered what happened to the other, but I just threw it in the back of my closet."

Brad grew impatient. "Yeah, yeah, touching story." He paused. "I thought it would be fun to leave it at the crime scene after I took care of that cocky little football jock I interviewed. Drake's little cut was all very innocent and I knew he would never be charged with anything, but it sure sent you all into a tizzy! Oh, Rachel, your face the day I showed you the photo. I enjoyed that." He laughed and took another step toward Daryl. "You know, Daryl, the day before I hacked up Stan the Man, I had a little conversation with him. He spilled the beans about your dad. Gave me every little detail about how Victor killed his wife. Ate some, left some, blah, blah, blah…poor guy. Imagine waking up one morning to find your wife's mutilated body lying next to you." Brad laughed again. "How did he *do* that? I mean, how does someone place a mutilated body next to you while you're sleeping, and you don't notice?" He shook his head and walked in a circle, keeping his eye on the three of them. "Drove poor Stan bat shit crazy. After they removed what was left of her from the house, he burned it down. Can you believe it? Burned his own house down. Crazy I tell ya!"

Rachel spoke in a whisper. "That poor man. Daryl, you should have told me. I've been wrong about everything."

Brad smiled. "This is so much fun." He waved the gun at Rachel and Drake again. "Aren't we having fun?" He fired a shot in their direction and it grazed Drake's thigh. He fell against him mom, gritting his teeth, and tried to hide the pain. He shook his head at the shadow in the corner.

Rachel pulled her bag off her shoulder and reached inside to find the knife while Brad was distracted with his own laughter. She unwrapped it and pulled it out. Brad looked over to see her holding it in front of her.

"Do you really think that knife will compete with my gun, Rachel?"

She pulled Drake behind her as she stood. "I'll plant this knife in you before you can pull the trigger."

"I doubt that, but let's test the theory, shall we?" He pulled the trigger as she threw. She pulled Drake down on top of the box as the bullet whizzed past. She looked up to see Brad struggling to remove the knife from his upper arm. He wiggled it back and forth, then in circles, creating a large hole in his arm. Blood and small pieces of flesh gushed from the wound and down his forearm. He gave a final grunt and pulled the knife free.

"Good throw, Rach!" He held the butt of the gun against the wound. "Do you know how hard it is to pull a knife out of bone? Good thing I've had a lot of practice."

Daryl rushed him and fought for the gun. It was slippery from the blood oozing from Brad's wound, and he tried to get a solid grip on it. Daryl pulled the gun down toward the floor and a shot went off, hitting Brad in the leg. He stumbled back against the wall as Daryl took possession of the gun.

"You're the son of a suspected cannibal. I'll cry self-defense. You'll never get away with it, Daryl."

"Actually, he will," Rachel said as she stepped forward with a recorder in her hand. "We have everything we need on tape. You don't think I ever go anywhere without this, do you? I hit record before I ever walked into the building."

Brad dropped to his knees, feeling light headed from the loss of blood. Daryl walked to him slowly and pushed him over. He turned to Rachel. "Cops are pulling up outside. I've been working with them the whole time. I told them to give me thirty minutes, then come. I'm sorry, but I thought you'd be the one they were carting off."

"Looks like we all misjudged this one. It's not going to be easy to get past this, you know. We need to work on our communication skills."

He nodded as police officers came up the stairs. They looked at Daryl and down at Brad. Rachel handed them the recorder. "Brad's your man. Everything you need is on this tape." She turned and walked down the stairs.

"Mom?"

She turned to face her son, who was having his leg looked at by an officer. "I'm really sorry."

She nodded with tears in her eyes. "Yeah, me too honey." She walked down the stairs. An officer caught up with her as she reached her car.

"You should have your head looked at."

She laughed, "You have no idea how right you are." She got in her car and drove away.

The next morning Daryl and Drake waited by the front door while Rachel carried her last bag to her car. Drake leaned against the frame of the door. "She won't even talk to us."

Daryl put his arm around his son. "Give her some time to work through this. We did accuse her of being a murderer."

"Yeah, well, she thought the same about both of us and we're handling it. At least we're trying to talk to her about it. She's just running away."

"For now, let her run. I think we could all use some time."

Rachel walked back to the front door and gave them both hugs goodbye. "I'm not sure when I'll be back."

Daryl simply nodded. Drake gave her a dirty look, but in his mind, tried to understand. She turned, walked to her car, and drove away.

Daryl sighed and looked down at his son's leg. "By the way, how are you feeling?"

He shrugged. "I'll live."

They walked back into the house and stood before the tree. Drake bent down and picked up a gift. "She didn't even take them with her."

"We'll put them away in case she ever comes back."

"Do you think she will?"

Daryl narrowed his eyes, deep in thought. "Yeah, I think she will." He reached down and pulled one of Drake's gifts from under the tree. "Ready to open them or do you want to wait?"

"No. I think we should open them now. In spite of everything that's happened, this Christmas is a turning point."

Daryl sat on the couch across from the tree. "Yes, you're right, Son, it is. Next year will be different." He took the gift that Drake offered. "Next year will be better."

Drake came and sat by his dad. "Merry Christmas, Dad."

"Merry Christmas, Son."

"You're handling this very well. If my wife just walked out on Christmas Day, I'd be freaking out."

Daryl chuckled. "Trust me; I'm as upset as you are. Remember, we all have our demons to contend with. It's how we deal with them that makes us the people we are. I've learned how to deal, Drake. As painful as life can be, I've learned how to deal."

"I love you, Dad. Thanks for dealing."

Daryl gave him a hug, and they sat on the couch and opened their gifts as Rachel made her way back to Seattle.

# 6 Months Later

"You know, June is a beautiful month in Montana." Rachel laughed at Daryl as they walked through the town square, hand in hand. They stopped and he kissed her lightly on the forehead. "I'm glad you're back."

She lowered her head. "I'm sorry I left the way I did, but I had to get my head on straight. After everything that happened and all those years of torment, I had to get away from it all."

"I understand. That's why I let you go. I knew you'd be back." He paused. "Seattle's been good to you."

"Yes, it felt good to go back, and six months of therapy didn't hurt." She bit her lip slightly. "Please, tell me the shadow is gone."

"I haven't seen the shadow of my father in months." He kissed her forehead again. She had a scar from the hit she took from the pipe. They all had scars to deal with. Some were visible, some were not. Drake ran up with an ice cream.

"Here, Mom! You're favorite flavor."

She took it and hugged her son. "Thank you, sweetheart!"

He wrapped his arm around hers. "So, you're here to stay, right?"

"Yes, honey, I'm here to stay." She pointed across the street to the local florist. "I'd like to get some flowers to put on Stan and Evelyn's graves."

Daryl nodded. "I think that's a great idea."

As they walked across the street, she glanced at Cromwell Creek's newspaper office. Daryl noticed her eyeing it. "Miss the place?"

"Not really."

"They could still use a good editor."

She laughed. "Thank you, but I think I've had my fill of Cromwell Creek's news."

They all laughed as they entered the florist.

Brad sat in his solitary cell. He'd got himself in trouble again for biting fellow inmates. He tried to explain to the guards that they just tasted so good, but they weren't buying it, and this solitary cell might as well of had his name plate on the door.

The shadow crept in between the cracks of the door. He was used to its presence, but this time, the shadow spoke; its disembodied voice filled the room.

"Well, well, back again, Brad?"

He crouched in the corner of the small room. The shadow had never spoken to him before and he was scared as hell. Normally, when the shadow appeared, it only played tricks on him. It especially enjoyed turning the food on his tray into human body parts. Arms, legs, internal organs; once he could have sworn he'd seen a human eyeball floating in his soup. But this time, the shadow spoke and called him by name.

"You can't ignore me. Silence is what I love most. I thrive on it."

"Go away! I'm not afraid of you."

Laughter filled the room. "Of course, you are. You're the biggest coward I know. I tried to make peace with what I did, but you just couldn't let it go. You wanted it, you got it, Brad."

The sound of muscle pulling away from bone filled the room. Tendons snapped and popped. Bones broke. Then chewing, slurping, and biting sounds followed. They filled the room in deafening volumes. Brad covered his ears and tried to mute the sounds with his own screaming. No matter how hard he pressed his hands to his head, the sounds were there. He jumped up and started running around in circles in his cell.

"Stop! Stop!"

Through the cannibalistic sounds, the voice of Victor Cromwell bellowed. "You'll never escape me. You wanted me, you got me."

Brad ran and ran in circles; everyday he would run, but the shadow of Victor Cromwell would make damn sure he never escaped.

The Cross
Examining

By Chad
Lutzke

Chad lives in Battle Creek, MI. with his wife and children where he works as a medical language specialist. For over two decades, he has been a contributor to several different outlets in the independent music and film scene including articles, reviews, and artwork. Chad loves music, rain, sarcasm, dry humor, and cheese. He has a strong disdain for dishonesty and hard-boiled eggs. Though he's bothered continuously by his family and friends to paint more, he claims his perfectionism has ruined any therapeutic value it once held and now finds its calming effect likened to that of bathing in a pool of piranha with bologna stapled to his legs. For now, and hopefully into the distant future, Chad uses writing as his creative outlet. He is a regular contributor to Horror Novel Reviews, and you can find his work in Shadows & Light #3 & #4 as well as various websites. Chad will also be releasing his own short story horror anthology early 2015. You can find him lurking around the following websites

Facebook Author page: www.facebook.com/authorchadlutzke

Amazon Author page: www.amazon.com/author/chadlutzke

Horror Novel Reviews Facebook page: www.facebook.com/ HorrorNovelReviews

# The Cross Examining
## By Chad Lutzke

Ever invite a vampire over for Christmas dinner? Yeah, well my mom did and it nearly got us all killed. Forget every vampire movie you've ever seen. Toss the "rules" you *thought* you knew about them. Most are true, but let me teach you about the ones that aren't and about the ones you've never heard before. I know them all and lived to tell about it.... all because of Christmas.

First I have to tell you about beautiful Angela. Angela was my best friend's older sister. They lived right next door to us. I could spend plenty of time using various metaphors and similes describing how gorgeous Angela is and how I've been in love with her since even before I hit my teen years, but none of that really matters because outside of yelling to my best friend: "Johnny! Phone's for you!" or "Johnny! Your friend is here!" she never much acknowledged me. I'd seen enough movies to know one day I'd get over her but for now I was utterly smitten. She was the "older woman" I longed for as a hormonally-charged teenager. Johnny knew about my attraction to his sister but never understood it. "Why, man? She's a prude," he'd say.

Angela had gone away for her first year of college. Christmas vacation had begun and she was due back home for the holiday right on Christmas Eve. My parents were close friends with Johnny's parents and had lived next to each other even before either of us was born. The tradition started when we were toddlers that we would spend all of Christmas Eve together eating a huge meal in one of our houses alternating each year. This year it would be my house. My mom had spent the last week preparing, decorating, shopping, and stressing; my house laden with the reminder of Christ's birth. Instead of reindeer, Santa, shiny bulbs, and tinsel, my mother made it her calling to excessively adorn the house as though Mary and Joseph themselves were coming, savior in tow. This was something she took great pride in. It wouldn't be until that year that I would actually welcome my mother's choice in holiday decor.

The day of Christmas Eve that year I had just finished my chores when Johnny called. I half expected him to. Like nearly every other day, we'd find ourselves spending the day riding bikes, building forts, or just daydreaming on our backs under the sun. The winter months were no less fun; many a hill would be ridden and snowballs tossed. It was good to be young and on Christmas vacation.

Johnny sounded distressed on the phone. "Ry, you're not gonna believe it."

"What? What is it?" His tone had me concerned.

"Meet me." And with that, he hung up.

Across the street was an empty field void of any trees, save for right in the middle where the land dipped down. That whole area was surrounded by trees. We called it Druid's Pond. Druid's Pond was a museum of two generations of eroded forts in various stages of decay. Although years ago it did hold water, it was now bone dry with plenty of trees to climb and rocks to sit on. A large handful of the trees still held remnants of scrap wood nailed to the trunks to form steps often leading up to rickety platforms enclosed by makeshift railings. It was the perfect place for a couple of teenagers to escape.

By the time I got to Druid's Pond, Johnny was already there seated on our favorite rock; one large enough to seat the two of us comfortably with no fear of crowding each other. He sat Indian style rocking anxiously back and forth.

"What's up, Johnny? You're mom getting all stressed out again? I swear that woman can turn a good day bad."

Johnny stopped rocking and looked at me with as about a serious look as he could muster. "My sister is gonna die and so are we.... and so are you. We're all gonna die! Well, not die, but you know, *die*!"

He managed to confuse and concern me even more. "Uhh, actually, no, I don't know. I take it this is not about your mom's holiday breakdowns."

Johnny started rocking again. "Undead, man! We're gonna die but not die. Like join the dark side. You see what I'm sayin'?"

"You mean like zombies?" I mocked him, putting my arms out in front of me stumbling toward him over the rocks and dirt. "Braaaaiiiins!" I fell down laughing. You had to know Johnny. He was a hypochondriac with the state's largest collection of horror comics, and the two weren't mixing well right now. "Garbage in, garbage out as Mom always says." He knew I was referring to his obsession with the comics.

"Ry, I'm being serious here. It's my sister's boyfriend."

"Wait! Your sister has a boyfriend?" This got me to stop laughing. He was right. This was serious. My heart sank a little. "How long they been goin' out? Maybe she doesn't really like him. Maybe she's just like one of them gold diggers, just waiting for a real man to come along." I said as I puffed my chest out, half serious.

"Not now, Ry. Look at me. Look at my face. Do I look like I'm in the mood to deal with your fantasies?"

"No, you're right. Let's deal with *your* fantasies." I said sarcastically. "Okay, so your sister's boyfriend." I nearly choked on the word boyfriend. "He's a zombie and you're afraid he wants your brains and your flesh and your mom and your dad and your dog and your shoes and your...."

"Not funny, man! And I never said anything about a zombie. He's not a zombie. He's a vampire."

I tried my hardest to hold back but there was no use. My tightened lips couldn't hold the beast of a laugh fighting its way out and winning. My lips flapped making a fart noise ejecting spittle in all directions followed by a full on laugh that erupted in a loud, exhaustive gust. Johnny was not amused. He sat glaring at me.

Forcing myself to cut the healthy laugh short, I replied to Johnny's last statement. "Okay man, details. Let's hear them. Her boyfriend not showing up in the bathroom mirror?" I started to chuckle again but successfully held most of it back. Snot nearly shot out my nose in the attempt.

"It's not like that. That's a fallacy."

"A what?"

"It's not true. The whole vampires and mirrors thing. It doesn't work like that. That's all a myth."

"Yeah, myth is right." I started to laugh once more.

Johnny shook his head. "Angela brought him home for the Christmas Eve meal. He's cold. He's pale. He smells like coconuts, wears sunglasses, and he just stood at the door until my dad welcomed him in."

"So, a polite albino with good hygiene standing in 30-degree weather who isn't a fan of being snow blind and you come up with vampire?"

Johnny's voice turned stern. "He wasn't being polite. He wouldn't come into the house because he couldn't. He wouldn't budge. He just stood there until my dad invited him in."

I stared blankly at Johnny waiting for him to continue. Evidently I was missing something.

"Ry, vampires can't enter someone's house unless they are specifically invited in by the owner."

My stare continued.

"And like an hour later after my mom had made some cookies, he handed me one and his hand touched mine. He was still cold. You know how warm my mom keeps that house. And the coconut smell; he was wearing sunscreen. It's December. Explain that, Ry!"

I'd never seen him so serious before. I had to hand it to him though; he definitely had done his homework.

"He's in my house, Ry! Right now! Invited right in!"

"You're being for real aren't you? I mean, you're completely convinced. I'm sorry, Johnny, but you can't really expect me to buy this. Come on let's go to your place.  We'll get some of those cookies you're talking about and maybe say hi to your sister."

Johnny hopped off the rock and grabbed my arm. "Okay, but before we get there you just gotta know, Ry. Angela isn't the same.  She's under this guy's spell!"

"It's called love, Johnny.  It'll do that.  Your sister does that to me right here."  I closed my eyes, sighed, and put my hand over my heart.  I peeked at him with one eye hoping to get a smile, but he was too distraught so I humored him a little.  "Okay, so Angela's a vampire now?"

"No, he can't hurt her.  At least I don't think he can.  When a vampire chooses a life mate there's a process.  He can't just go turning her like some regular victim.  It's a courting thing.  I'm not real sure on it.  I just know if Angela is his choice for a mate then she's safe for now.  The problem is she has no idea she's in any danger and his hold on her will only become stronger."

"Come on, buddy" I said grabbing him by the shoulder.  "Let's get a *bite* to eat."  I opened wide as I said it.  My teasing him didn't make things any better.

"Again, not funny, Ry!"

As we walked back to Johnny's house I watched him bite his nails, flaring his nostrils with each feeding.  It wasn't hard to tell he was completely lost in thought.  It was hard to watch.  I felt like I was witnessing a friend literally lose his mind right before me.  When we got back to Johnny's house I could see a slick black Mustang in the driveway.  The paint glistened as though it was still wet.  It must have been the boyfriend's car.  It was impressive, I had to admit.  Across the street from Johnny's house, Mr. Bell was bringing in some groceries and spotted the car.  He took a moment to let us know his appreciation for it.

"Wooowee!  Look at that beauty!  That a V8 in there? I'll bet that baby smokes on the freeway!"

Johnny stopped walking and spit out a fingernail. "I'm not really sure, Mr. Bell.  It's not mine."

I kept facing forward looking at the car.  I was not a fan of Mr. Bell.  Most people on the street weren't.  Every neighborhood had that one guy and Mr. Bell was him; even my cat never wandered over there. Mr. Bell's wife had left him years ago and he's lived alone ever since. He deserves it if you ask me. My mom always told me not to slander, but I'd seen Mrs. Bell more than once run out of that house crying, and if his behavior outside the house in any way hinted at it, then I'd hate to know what was going on behind closed doors.

"Whose is it? No way that's your old man's. He wouldn't know how to handle a sexy thing like that!" He yelled across the street.

"It's my sister's....boyfriends."

He liked using that word even less than I liked hearing it.

"Lucky kid! I'll bet that's all it takes for your sister to skip them bases if you know what I mean." Followed by a perverse belly laugh.

"Yeah, ha! Johnny half mocked him without him knowing.

"Hey Ryan! Yer mom got all her Jesus freak stuff put up for the year?" And with that he laughed even harder and walked inside.

Johnny turned back toward me.

"Okay listen. Whatever you do, Ry, do *not* invite Angela's boyfriend over in any way; not even small talk about just hanging out."

"Johnny, we're all eating at my place tonight."

"Yeah, I know. We'll have to think of something. Unless of course you'd like to wake up in the morning drained of your blood and part of the undead army."

"Depends. Do I get to drive a car like that?" I pointed to the Mustang. I don't know what was getting older, Johnny insisting vampires were real or my making fun of him. I decided to finally lay off and give my best friend the benefit of the doubt; emphasis on doubt.

"Remember, no inviting him!" Johnny said desperately.

Keeping my mouth shut was proving to be rather difficult. Just as we were approaching the front door to Johnny's house, it opened and out walked Angela followed by what I had to assume was her boyfriend. Johnny's description was on par, but actually seeing him was like looking at a picture of mountain scenery on a calendar versus actually standing at the top of said mountain looking out across the rest of the world. There was a certain awe, and I was instantly hit with an awkwardness that I couldn't tell if it came from seeing Angela for the first time since summer or pure intimidation while in the presence of her boyfriend. He emitted a cool yet distressing and mysterious aura. Johnny had failed to mention his nearly white hair. The smell of coconut mixed with Angela's voice broke any fixation I had on him.

"Hey Ry! This is my man, Julian."

Her man. My stomach turned and I nearly rolled my eyes. He reached out his hand. I stalled, but instinct—and maybe a little bit of intimidation—took over and I greeted him with a handshake. Johnny was right. He was freezing. I instantly felt uneasy and even a little bit paranoid. I felt like I couldn't let on that I knew anything. And knew *what* exactly? That my best friend thinks that chilled coconut albinos are the devil's minions?

Suddenly Johnny just blurted it out. "How old are you, Julian?"

"My gosh, Johnny. That is so rude." Angela contended.

"Ha! It's okay, Ang. Older than you, buddy." He mussed Johnny's hair as he said it, adding to the intimidation.

"Well, boys. We're off for a walk. How about you kids go play in one of your forts and leave the grownups alone." Angela waved at someone behind me.

"Come on, baby." Angela spoke to Julian. "Let me introduce you to Mr. Bell. I think you'll like him."

"Ang, are you serious? You hate Mr. Bell. Johnny said.

"I think Julian will like him, and Mr. Bell is so lonely."

That didn't sound like Angela at all. She disliked the guy more than any of us. Johnny was right again. I watched them walk by me and down the driveway as Julian pulled a cigarette out and lit it. Johnny grabbed me by the coat and tugged at me to go inside. We ran back to my house and once safely in my room, Johnny began an interrogation.

"Do you see it? Do you see now what I'm talking about? It's gotta be obvious to you now. Please tell me I'm not alone here, Ry."

I couldn't believe that I was even considering it but I was; heavily. I reflected on my whole outlook before and after meeting Julian. That in itself creeped me out. As farfetched as any of this may have seemed, I was young. There would come a day I would be yelling at kids to get off my lawn; a day when I would be filled with pessimism and unimaginative thinking; stuck in my own ways brought on by personal life experiences, regret, and bitterness at the world, but for now I wanted to revel in my youth; to use my imagination and have fun with what life was giving me right now.

"Yes, Johnny!" I spoke right to Johnny's eyes. "I see it. I see it big time and you're right. He's a vampire. I believe you." I wasn't just trying to be convincing and Johnny knew it. I *was* convinced.

We spent the next hour or two going over what we knew of vampires, which apparently wasn't as much as we thought we did. The internet was filled with myths and facts. We had learned a handful of things that were just not true about vampires. As Johnny had already said, mirrors were not a problem for vampires and neither were stakes. That was all the work of fictional literature and Hollywood. The only way they could cease to exist was from decapitation or complete exposure to sunlight, which brings me to the sunscreen. Daylight was indeed lethal to vampires, but centuries of scientific advancement led them to your average sunscreen as an adequate block against the sun's potentially deadly rays. Garlic, we learned, was nothing more than an irritating attractant. They really found the smell no more repulsive than your average person; however, they had a much more keen awareness of it. If anything, it just led the vampire straight to anyone who was a believer in vampirism. Seeing a wreath of garlic hanging over a door or around someone's neck was a sure sign to a vampire that their presence was made aware of, and in turn they normally would end the person's life for fear of the victim sharing their observation with others.

We also learned that vampires were indeed immortal and that they could turn others into vampires but only once or twice per year. Their blood had to be pure during the process with no recent kills and their victim had to drink from the vampire's own blood, usually while under the trance of the vampire. Other than turning others, vampires would only prey on the living in order to seek revenge, if they felt threatened, and to retain their physical age, which was the age they themselves were when originally turned. Apparently Julian was in his late teens to early 20s when he became one himself. There was no telling how old he truly was, but the thought of potentially centuries of life experience and knowledge was quite an intimidating weapon.

One other interesting fact we read was the use of salt. It is written that vampires avoid it at all costs, and that you can literally form a line with it that they will not cross. That alone could be an excellent defense on making sure our Christmas Eve dinner remained bloodsucker free. I had to admit, though I was scared, all the research, planning, and discussion actually got me excited. I was prepared to protect my family and of course, Angela.

It was obvious what our next move was; surround the house with salt. Johnny and I headed downstairs. The smell of freshly baked cookies and slowly cooking turkey penetrated my nostrils deeper with each stair taken. There was something about those traditional smells that gave me a sudden boost of courage. As we approached the pantry door, my mother's suspicions arose.

"What are you guys up to? You're not taking any more of my food to one of your little forts."

"No Mom. We're looking for the salt."

"The salt?" She looked puzzled but then broke into a grin. "You mean the rock salt? Aww... Are you boys going to get rid of some of that ice out there on the front steps? That'll really please your father when he gets home."

We hadn't even thought of rock salt; all the better. Johnny spoke up before I had a chance to. "Yes, Ma'am. We don't need any broken hips out there tonight on this fine Christmas Eve." It sounded fake. I was embarrassed for him immediately, but my mother seemed to buy it.

"Well, God bless your sweet little hearts. It's in the garage right by the door. Oh, and Ryan, when you're out doing that stop by Johnny's and tell Angela and her friend it'll be in about two hours. I feel bad. I told them only one hour and this turkey has at least another 90 minutes to go. This old oven doesn't want to work like it used to. Thanks honey."

We simultaneously stopped our trek to the garage door. I think our mouths were both open. "Wait, Mom. Did you talk to Angela today?"

"Yes I did. She's so sweet. I saw her and her boyfriend out in the driveway when I was getting the mail. He's handsome....different, but handsome." She trailed off.

"Mom, did you invite them over for dinner?"

"Honey, we've been doing this for years. She knows the routine. She'll be here. You still have that little crush on her don't you?" The way she said it made me feel several years younger. If she was standing closer she would have pinched my cheek while saying it.

"Did you invite them? Did you invite Julian? Did you ask him to dinner tonight?" I tried to hide the panic in my voice.

Confusion showed on her face. "Well, no. I didn't *ask* him."

Johnny and I both let out the breath we'd been holding.

"He asked if he could join us, and I told him he was more than welcome to come over for dinner tonight. I mean, he *is* with Angela, ya know."

It was all we needed to hear. My family and I had officially become one of Julian's menu options. While my mother's attention was pulled away by the buzz of a cooking timer, Johnny and I headed out to the garage. The rock salt was exactly where my mother said it would be. We each grabbed a 10-pound bag and headed to the front. There were no words exchanged between Johnny and I. After the lengthy discussion in my room, we knew exactly what needed to be done. We were completely synchronized. Even as we headed out the garage door, I went left and Johnny went right; without a word. Before a single pellet of salt hit the ground, we both looked around for any sign of Julian. If we were going to be seen by a vampire building a moat of salt around the house, we may as well be wearing garlic hats too.

After making sure we were in the clear, Johnny and I carefully made a solid trail of rock salt around the entire perimeter of the house doubling up in front of the windows and tripling up in front of the doors. To avoid any further parental suspicions, we made sure to clear the steps and front walk of any ice and snow. We shook the rest of the contents of the rock salt bags on the front doorstep, then looking at each other gave a nod of approval; synchronized; without a word.

Johnny and I found ourselves with plenty of time and nothing to do but wait. Wait on the arrival of an evil, undead, immortal make a scene in front of the house where it would be revealed what he truly was, at which point Johnny and I would tackle him into the snow and separate his tropical-fruit-smelling ivory head from the rest of him via hatchet, while neighbors and family cheered for us just moments before they picked us up on their shoulders celebrating us as great conquerors of evil. At least that's the scenario that we had come up with. We knew it might go down differently but were hoping at the very least Angela would see Julian for what he really is.

Nearly two hours had passed while we sat in my bedroom. The time was spent with countless "what ifs" and going over every possible scenario we could imagine with our young and excited—yet scared—minds. We agreed that given our circumstances the only thing we could do was watch and wait. The possibility of Julian being nothing more than a freak show with poor taste in cologne was still relevant, so just running at him right now with axe in hand wasn't an option. Watch and wait it was.

My room was on the corner of the house on the top floor. Two different windows acted as our lookout posts; one faced the front of the house while the other faced Johnny's. We sat on patrol as we talked; each of us fixed in a concentrated stare out our designated windows awaiting any sign of Julian and Angela. As the time went by, the scents from the kitchen grew stronger. Every half hour brought a new aroma mixed in with the nearly-done turkey. I had never been so hungry before yet so lacking in appetite. My stomach was not fond of the watch-and-wait approach we were forced to endure and seemed to be caught up in some bipolar fit of indecisiveness.

"Ry! There he is!" I nearly threw up as a reaction. I hurried over to the window facing Johnny's house. There was beautiful Angela hand in hand with the enemy as they walked to the car I both loved and hated. Julian opened his car door, reached inside, and grabbed a pack of smokes from within. I found a smile gradually replacing the frown I wore for the past two hours as I thought of that cigarette being his last; ready for execution. The frown returned again knowing there was not much just Johnny and I would ever be able to do, but I still had hope that all would be revealed causing a chain reaction of chaos resulting in, at the very least, a capture of Angela's undead Romeo.

We sat in silence watching Julian fill his undead lungs with nicotine. Did he even feel the effects of it? So many questions about vampires that I prefer remain unanswered. I wanted my experience with them to be quick and a one-time deal only. Julian flicked his cigarette in a pile of snow, grabbed Angela's hand and started walking toward my house.

"Let's go!" Johnny grabbed my sleeve and tugged at it as he bolted out of my room. We both scurried down the first set of stairs to the landing and watched the front door through the wooden railing in a straight shot safely from there. If everything worked according to our plan, Julian wouldn't pass our force field of salt and the doorbell would never ring. I could see my mother from our hiding spot. While setting the table for our guests, she must have spotted Angela and Julian through the window approaching the front, because I saw her quickly set down the silverware and rushes toward the door. "Ryan! Johnny! Angela is here." She yelled.

We watched as my mother opened the door. She had it open before they even started up the front steps. "Hi kids! Merry Christmas! Come on in!"

Angela led the way up the steps. Julian stopped at the top step and looked down. He saw the salt. He shook his head, and I swear he chuckled to himself. We watched in horror as he stepped completely over the thick line of salt and into my house.

My mother yelled for us again. "Ryan! Johnny!"

I whispered to Johnny. "The salt is another myth! We're screwed. We are *so* screwed. He knows we know! I can tell!"

Apparently my whisper was too loud because my mother turned and called us out. "There they are. Come on little ninjas. It's time for dinner. Johnny, Angela says your folks will be here in about 10 minutes, and Ryan your dad is on his way home as we speak."

If I wasn't so afraid of Julian's enthusiasm for blood transfusions, I would have died from embarrassment right there. We came out from behind our stair rail blinder and trudged down the stairs. It was a walk of shame and fear. The kind of walk a man heading to the gallows would experience. My mother made small talk for the next few minutes while Julian charmed her with compliments concerning the aroma of the food, her beauty, and her well-kept house. My bipolar stomach was just given another reason to remind me it wasn't happy.

"How about we get you guys settled in the living room until the others get here. There's a nice fire going in there. Oh, and Angela I've been waiting all week to show someone our tree. We went with a purple theme this year. Just wait until you see it." My mother said while leading them from the foyer.

Johnny and I followed along into the room like two timid puppies. We traded worried glances. Neither of us knew what to do at this point. Our watch and wait turned into wait and die. Just before we stepped around to the living room, Julian looked at me and smiled. His smile spoke a thousand words about how he knew, and about how my life would soon come to an end as a result. It wasn't just a warning in that smile but a promise. Johnny saw it too. I nearly grabbed Johnny and ran until I saw the look on Julian's face change from satisfaction to horror. He looked as though he had seen something unspeakable; as though he felt genuinely feared for his wellbeing. I looked in the direction of his terror just as Johnny had elbowed me. It was my mother's decorations. The large nativity scene, the crucifixes on the wall, the two dozen purple crosses hanging on the tree in place of your usual bulbs. Of course! The cross was a reminder to the vampire of their eventual eternal damnation. They couldn't be around it. The internet had been wrong about the salt and apparently it was wrong about the crucifix as well. Everything we had read alluded to the fact that the vampire's fear of the crucifix was untrue, yet here we were witnessing an ambush of Christ upon one of the unholy.    Julian's eyes streaked red with thick bloodshot and began to water.  The corners of his mouth quickly filled with a white foam as he clutched his throat and dropped to his knees.  Both my mother and Angela swung around to find Julian suffering before the image of Christ on the eve of the savior's birthday.  I looked at Johnny whose grin was ridiculous in size; mine matched it.

The front door opened and it was Johnny's parents. "We're here! Sorry we're a little late, Helen.  Al couldn't find the gift he'd bought Ted."  From where they stood they couldn't see the defeat happening before us.

Angela—panic filled—pleaded with her weakened and vulnerable boyfriend.  "Julian!  Honey, are you okay? What's happening?  What can I do?  Someone please help!"

Shockingly, my mother stood there for a second before responding.    She looked unfazed and almost irritated.    She bent down to and made eye contact with Julian.  Her face was stern and bold.  "Julian, listen to me. Are you allergic to cats?  Is that it?"

Julian looked confused as though he didn't understand what she had said, but he eventually did and nodded his head.

Johnny's parents, curious about the commotion, ran to the living room.

"Let's get him outside, everyone."  My mother calmly said.

Johnny's dad and Angela helped Julian up and led him to the front door.  Julian grabbed the door handle and let himself out without hesitation.  Once outside he violently kicked at the tiny wall of salt.  He pulled at his leather coat as though straightening himself out; spit onto the ground the foam he had produced, rubbed his eyes, and began to run his fingers through his hair.  He was embarrassed. "Forgive me, everyone.  Mrs. Young's is correct.  I am extremely allergic to felines.  I'm afraid I will be unable to attend your wonderful dinner tonight ma'am."  He wouldn't look at my mother while saying it.  Physically, he looked completely unscathed—a far cry from the unholy mess that was falling apart just seconds ago—there was shame and fear in both his voice and mannerisms.

Angela consoled him. "You never told me you were allergic to cats. I'm so sorry. I would have told you they had one, sweetie."

Angela's mother started in. "I'm so sorry, dear. Perhaps we can bring a plate home later tonight for you."

Angela interrupted. "Thanks, Mom, but I think Julian and I will just take Mr. Bell up on his offer. He invited us to join him earlier and you know how lonely he gets at Christmas."

I could almost feel the unbelieving stares Angela was receiving in response. Johnny elbowed me again. I didn't catch on right away that Mr. Bell had invited them over....to his house.

"Mr. Bell? As in, across-the-street, wife-beater, pervert, Mr. Bell? "Angel's mother retorted.

"It's Christmas, Mom. He's all alone."

For fear of looking heartless during the Christmas season, Angela's mother quickly changed her tone. "Okay dear. Please don't be long. I suppose everyone deserves a little Christmas cheer."

And just like that, Angela and Julian headed toward Mr. Bell's. A real life vampire was just brought to his knees spewing foam and tears right in my living room and now we're headed in to eat a turkey dinner. I kept thinking about my mother's reaction to Julian's unholy seizure. It didn't faze her at all; almost as though she expected it. While the others sat warming by the fire in the living room, I snuck off to help my mom finish setting the table.

"Did you know, Mom?" It was a risky question, but her response surprised me. She took my hands and looked in my eyes. "You're safe, honey. Don't ever worry about him ever again. You'll always be safe."

She did know; but for how long? There was a history here I was unaware of, but I didn't care. I believed her and felt safer than I ever had. I hugged her hard. I wanted to cry but refrained and kept my composure. Before I let go of the hug I asked her one more question. "What about Mr. Bell?"

"That's between him and Jesus, honey, and right now I don't think Mr. Bell is a fan of Jesus *or* his freaks. Now let's get full."

I grabbed the extra plate and silverware Mom had set and put them away. My stomach went manic, and I was more than ready for Mom's Christmas Eve dinner.

The Hobo and The Layman

By Victor George Matak

Victor Matak lives in Toronto, Ontario. His poetry and prose have featured in, or are forthcoming, in publications such as Sterling Magazine, The Gap Tooth Madness; Crack the Spine Literary Magazine, Red Paint Hill Poetry Journal and Review, IN MY BED Magazine, Hilt Magazine, Poet's Digest Magazine, In-Flight Magazine, Bloody Sexy Erotic Horror Anthology and others.

# The Hobo and the Laymen
## By Victor George Matak

Angel's mom had dropped us off at the corner of Granville and Broadway where we stood with portentous ass cracks, sweating like the construction workers outside the sandwich shop, and we both knew that if our mannerisms weren't well-placed that one of the patrol cars would drive up and mistake us for two hobos and maybe arrest us. We were standing outside Wickham's Convenience Store, hoping to see if we could convince one of the business men to buy us a pack of cigarettes with the money we had stolen out of Angel's mother's purse when she had run back into the house, briefly, to grab a book – D.H. Lawrence's *Women in Love*. I had never read the book, nor did I want to but Angel told me he had spent five minutes masturbating to one of the passages though he hadn't come. It was erotic, he told me, and had been banned like Henry Miller's *Tropic of Cancer* though neither of us had read that either.

"It's a roman a clef," Angel said.
"Are you speaking Latin?"
"I don't know. Can you speak Latin?"
"Do I look Latin?"
"There aren't even Latin people anymore."
"Yes, there are. What do you think Italians are?"
"Italians."
"No, they're – "
"Fine. I guess I'm speaking Latin."
"Let me ask you another question."
"What?"
"Why are you even speaking Latin?"
'Good question.

Angel was a liturgical fellow. This meant that on weekends he would spray graffiti onto the neo-gothic churches of the local university campus or tactfully measure his new pair of Nikes before placing them on the priest's doorstep, lighting them on fire. It was either this, or dog shit, he would tell me. He called us the Two Laymen and I understood this in a derogatory sense but he insisted on laymen being like an orbit, the solution to a difficult structural problem – that we were simple, organic.

"Are you saying we're stupid, then?" I had asked.

"No, that we're smarter."

"What do you mean?"

"It's easy for stupid people to act smart. If you're smart, the hardest thing you can do is act stupid. You see, this means we're smarter. We know everything. We don't need to pretend, you see? We're goddamn geniuses."

The day was red hot and it took us a few minutes to convince a grey-haired man in a dark gray suit to take our twenty dollars. His face was creased and tanned bronze and I thought maybe he had been a smoker before when, young like us, he had stood outside of stinky buildings relying on exhausted luck.

"I could get in a lot of trouble for this," he said.

"We're not cops, my man. Don't worry," Angel replied.

"I'm not worried."

After a few minutes of standing outside Wickham's, he came back outside with a pack of Marlborough lights though we asked for reds and smiled, broadly, and walked toward the intersection. Had it been a smirk, Angel would have said something but we were accustomed to this indifference. We never received our cigarette or alcohol change because we were in no position to ask. It was my money that we were spending with some odd dollars Angel would throw in when he could deceive his mom long enough to get them. But there was no use complaining because we had our smokes and were giddy like the male movie stars we never did believe in but found ourselves inexplicably wanting to make love to.

Outside the high school entrance, we tried hard to look poised so if any of the girls came by they would admire us. There was a poster of James Dean in my room though I hadn't seen any of his movies and we had mimicked the stance – tilted jaw, loose hips, disinterested look. The smokes were harsh but neither of us would confess it.

Cameron Goose, the principle, sauntered by with the lope of someone who has had his knee smashed in with a baseball bat and we hid behind a cubby in the brick work. We tried to deuce a second cigarette but couldn't. It was filling the lungs in a way that you don't want to acknowledge but can't escape the heave, the terse breathes that hurt.

Having nothing else to do, we headed to gym class only so that we could stand on the sidelines of the dodge ball game and pretend that we were too cool but we both knew that we wanted to play. It was fun to smote, hard, one of the jocks in the face or the pretty girls who hiked up their shorts so that the crease of their butts were rendered, juggling.

The gym locker rooms were small and dingy and you had to watch kids towel whip each other, fling their penises around – the sound of bone on bone – and laugh because it was fun to act like a homosexual though if you said something you would get a hard punch in the face.

Angel had a workman's penis. It was ruddy and sturdy – powerful in a sure way. It was like my own and I had never experienced that doubt so many other kids talked about in the gym locker rooms. We had shown off our manhood to each other innumerable times before. Once, Angel had tried to convince me to press my butt against his while he masturbated. I declined and he still brought it up like some kind of guilt-trip.

"It's a goddamn good penis," Angel said.

"Yours is good too."

"I know. But you got a fire-breather."

"A what?"

"A fire-breather. Like, you know those Japanese knights? They fight the dragons so they become the dragon."

"I've never heard that."

"It's in one of those Manga comics."

"Cool."

"Yeah, well, it's a good penis. I just call it how I see it."

There was Fort Hobo where he and I would burn the coiled branches off of trees and where to enter was to shout fuck! As loud as you could and to see the hidden birds scurry off and be bitter about the noise we caused. We came to Fort Hobo after school and, sometimes, on the weekends when I told my parents that I was at the local mall or trying to get a job. Here, we stashed the Smirnoff vodka bottles and the Palm Mall cigarettes and the two butterfly knives we had gotten out of the back end of a truck parked in the Indian Reserve. There was a ditch you had to cross and you didn't know you had crossed it until someone told you. You could fall into the ditch, you were liable to die. But no one ever did because no one was ever that flamboyant. The code was, Angel said, to keep it outlawed, a secret. That meant you had to be smart because if you opened your mouth, then the parents found out and then the teachers and the point of it was gone. Angel always spoke with the brusque way of a military commander though his voice was smooth and kind.

"It's the cigarettes," he said.

"What do you mean?"

"They're making me look old. And my voice is just about shot to smack."

"No it isn't. And you don't look old."

"Really, you sure?"

"Yes."

"Thanks, man."

The closest we ever got to being exposed was the night Brianna Hidgen first came, wearing a flower dress and yellow flat shoes and hair tied up in an amber ponytail. I knew Angel had a thing for her. We didn't say crush because that was an elementary school word. It was the desire, he called it. A real man, he said, was of the desire. He took a woman even if they said no because they really meant yes. All women said no, he said, and you could read about it in Cosmopolitan or in the books. It was like the dolphins that were forced to converge in packs so that they could have sex with the females. It was the same with Otters, Angel told me. We didn't call it rape because that was too severe. The big sin was being sexually frustrated. If you were sexually frustrated then you were stuck in eternal hell on earth.

"It's funny!" Brianna shouted.

"No, it isn't. Put the goddamn knife down," I said.

"Make me!"

"Watch out, man, she's nuts," and the knife cut near Angel's face and tilted downward, "Jesus Christ, you're in for a real treat."

I snatched Brianna's wrist before she could thrust the knife back into my stomach and wrestled it from her lame knuckles. Then, I flung the knife far into a patch of weeds and smacked Brianna hard across the face with a backhand movement. She sobbed, her tiny shoulders heaving up and down and Angel laughed: "Serves her right, the goddamn psychopath. No wonder your dad hit the hills running."

"He didn't leave," she said.

Brianna still had the gut defiance of someone conditioned to abuse and I admired anyone in those moments. I thought I might die in all the excitement, the speckled brilliance of the thrill.

"Go back to the convent you dirty spangler."

"Spangler?"

"Spangler, Hidgens. Fuck!"

The first time Angel and I asserted ourselves as real men, like those we had read online, or seen in television shows and heard from other kids at school, was in the summer before grade eight. We had been walking in the gravel playground of T.H. Ortons High School, an old, dilapidated, sketchy place where you rolled your eyes to make sure no one was going to spring up and jump you, take all your belongings and leave you mucked, bruised and gone of confidence. It had those red and blue painted swing sets, optimized constructive jungle gyms and little toy dump trucks that you sat on and used your hands to wheel, motion, and feel the authority of being in control, infallible and unquestioned. It had all the matter of an innocent place but I always felt an eerie, queasy sort of quality whenever I walked through it.

"You're superstitious," Angel said.

"And If I am?"

"Why?"

"Because."

"I think I'm getting cold sores."

"What do you mean?"

"Look at my mouth, it looks foul."

"That's vile."

"It's not so bad when you put tooth paste on. Dries it right out. If I get the pimples then I just splotch toothpaste on. Next morning, bang – gone. You should try it."

"Is it a pimple or a cold sore?"

"You've got a boil on your nose."

"Quit deflecting."

"Chrissake, that's Marxist."

"How so, Angel?"

"Don't use my first name."

"Mk, duntz' mcgee."

"What the fuck?"

We often found ourselves saying things that we had heard. "Osmosis," Angel called it. It was easier for us place things in this type of deferential reasoning than to acknowledge that we didn't know the meanings. We were terrified of being unattractive: *stupid*.

Earlier in the day, we had smoked marijuana out of my brother's purple glass pipe in Angel's back alley, tucked between a sloping garage and a chain link fence that stretched onto a dying, empty lawn. The pipe felt smooth along your hands. The carved ridges were something exceptional, unfixed when they passed the rough skin of your palms. You wanted to cup those ridges, exact some surety, some epiphany that the marijuana never did provide. So when a number of Indian men came from somewhere inside T.H. Ortons High (what we later decided was the outdoor basketball courts) and started yelling at us to 'get the fuck out of their country,' it seemed that the only rationale step for Angel and I to take was to respond, voluminously. There, we felt invincible. But, more than that, we felt hungry, angry for our own validation.

"Fuck you!"

"No! Fuck you!"

"This is our country, get the fuck out!"

"Your country? We're white, buddy. Are you fucked?" Angel screamed, his head lolling and his hands, outright, shaking fiercely.

"What you say, buddy? What he say buddy?!"

"Fuck! Fuck! Fuck!" I shouted. The inanity, the recycling of the word fuck seemed to me hypocrisy. Words lost potency when used so often, they shriveled and became adjunct, purposeless. I was eager for the fight and I did not want the episode to become childish and idiotic. I didn't know if Angel felt the same way, but he looked surly, mindful the way someone gets when they know the world beyond is missing, and the one in front is grim and mortal. The way someone gets when they consider death a viable consequence.

As they drew closer, Angel and I decided to take stock. The odds were slim. I felt that we had not done enough, at least not from what I had seen, to warrant the taunts we had just shouted. Then again, I always felt this way – some dark, rooted insecurity of performance. I had only fought once, discounting the inestimable times my older brother had beaten me, and I had suffered a broken nose and a sore jaw that persisted for a week.

"There's fourteen," I told Angel, fidgeting with the butterfly knife inside my sweatpants pocket.

"You sure?'

"I counted."

"Yes, but how well do you count?'

"Pretty well.

"Okay, how are we going to do this?"

"Do we have a choice?"

"Nope. We're fucked."

"Good luck."

"Good luck."

The first came fast, head ramming into Angel's stomach. I ducked to the side, and coiled my right arm and loosely slammed it towards a strong jaw that passed into my peripherals. Then, I noticed that the one Indian I had slugged was on the ground, hands clasped onto his face. I dove and cradled my knees around his neck and hit and hit and hit. I screamed and felt the red in my eyes, brimming, soon to implode. I smacked my hand and I hit and hit and hit unremittingly unremitting unremittingly. My fist was hard and bony and squeezed. The feel of a formidable bone, obstinate and then pliable. My hand raised and lowered, swinging unremittingly. I hit and hit until -

When I awoke, Angel was standing over me. His face scratched and smeared in blood, a purple bruise forming around his left eye. His shorn t-shirt, his arms scraped from the gravel and the torn hole in his jean shorts all looked like the outcome of some great belligerent chaos. The image of something you would never forget.

"Are you conscious or what?" Angel said.

"Yes."

"How's your head?"

"What do you think?"

"Yeah, well. You got dummied."

"Dummied?"

"It's a colloquialism."

"Give it a rest."

"Chrissakes. You're all girth."

"You're thick."

"Christ you're –"

"Whatever."

It was Angel who decided what was *real* and we thought it a gem – a moment of beautiful irony – when we discovered a homeless man slumbering a few minutes hike from our own hospice. Fort Hobo was a territorial place.

Often, you had to walk around a few times to ensure that no one else had made a claim. If they did, which never did happen, then you had to challenge them to a scrape. That was what we called fights – scrapes. If it was a real clean, long good fight then you would call it a brawl. We had kept tabs on the place ever since we had first uncovered it, in the middle of grade seven. Now, we were eighth graders freshly inducted into the high school scene.

There was something bizarre about the gizzard neck. The hobo was scraggly, and looked disgusted at us as we were at him. Above everything, he looked dizzy and there was that complacent look. The one you see when you've known it. When you've eaten too much at dinner or had a good make out with a girl and don't want to move. You are tired because you are made easy. There's nothing to do but accept and recoil from the fast pace of things. But the hobo looked beaten and entitled to a mound that was truncated in the fresh leaves constructed as a rooftop – a stick, either for walking or beating or riding. He was a pathetic creature, like someone crying or acting strong or the misappropriated instant where you look uninteresting. You wanted to spit on him.

Angel took out the lighter and flung it to the side. He walked up to the scraggly man and yanked on his dirty beard. There were leaves in the beard.

"Christ, old man. Dontcha gotta job?"

The old man was silent, existing only because he wasn't awake.

"Watcha gon doin be deaf, fer?"

"Angel, what the hell are you trying to imitate?"

"Imitate?"

"Yeah, that accent. What is it?"

"I'm like one of those confederates in the US."

"You sound Scottish."

"Alright then oui big lad."

"You're shite at accents."

"You're right."

He smacked the old man across the face and a second time under his nose and bloodied him. The leathery face, crumpled, did not move but the eyes were wistful and blue and looked blind.

"Take it easy, would you?"

"He's already dead, I'm sure of it."

"How do you know?"

"He's not breathing."

"He's breathing."

"Maybe a little but the old tit doesn't seem to understand anything."

"Maybe he's deaf."

"Maybe he's pretending."

"Could be blind or drunk."

"Maybe."

There was a gargling and I suddenly recalled that same gargling from my own mother, lying on the floor with a bottle of bleach next to her mouth. And I remembered the bread crumbs that she had tried to force into that mouth – timid and calm. My father had hoisted her emaciated frame into his arms and carried her into the bed. He had a limp, then. That was after he had been in the accident at the logging camp.

"There we go, how does that feel you crusty bucket?"

Angel had taken the hobos face and smeared it down into the dirt. He was undoing his pants and I turned away when the shit fell into the old man's hair, mangled and dirty.

"What a dirty old bird."

"Him?"

"What are you saying?"

"You just took a dump on that man's head. What did he do to you?"

"I guess you're right."

"Christ, Angel. Some things you don't do."

"Says who?"

"Use your goddamn head."

"I am and I make my own choices!"

The steal toed boots that Angel had got from his older brother who worked at a warehouse fell hard into the old man's head. There were fishing rods in the old man's home. And shards of glass, bait and the dank smell of piss and feces and gasoline.

"So help me god, Angel."

"What's that?"

"Where did you get that anyway?"

"My garage. It's been in my backpack this whole time. I'm surprised you didn't smell it."

"What are you doing with it?"

"I'm just kidding around. When did you get so pious?"

"Do you even know what that word means?"

"Eh, no."

"Don't you do whatever it is you're thinking of doing."

"You need to mellow out. Stop raging."

Just then, the match fell and lit up the body and he was sober and moaning, first, and then he screeched and I stood and watched. And it was a hideous sound. I did not try to stop it. I did not make to strike Angel. I did nothing until the smell was too much and I had to turn around.

I am in the Starbucks looking at her face. There is a London Fog placed on the table, near her long, slender hands. A twinge of red blush on her knuckles as a draft penetrates into the enclosed space. I feel my hand on the table as I sit down, hung-over. And I think how beautiful she looks, the figure that is not gaunt or loud but voluptuous and I cannot take my eyes off of her. This declarative creature is my lover. In a few minutes, I'll purchase a black coffee but I am adjusting my sore back and trying to make it comfortable in the wooden chair. She is a woman, not a girl. Years of callousness and insincerity has taught me the difference. Hindsight – she taught me the word. She is a student at the University. Why she's with me I don't know but that doesn't matter. And I see her brittle eyes and I think of Angel. Gone and gone.

"Tell me a secret," she asks.

"I've told you basically everything."

"You only say that, I want you to, really, tell me everything."

"There's nothing to tell that I haven't already told you."

"You're twenty four years old and you're telling me you have no secrets?"

"Nope. Sorry."

"How boring."

"Awe, shucks."

This Little Pissy

By Sandy Rozanski

My name is Sandra Rozanski. I am a poet who dabbles in short stories. I have been writing since I was eight years old and began with a passion for horror, those dark and stormy nights sort of thing. Somewhere along the way, though I continued to write, took a few courses and had a few poems published, I managed to marry and have a big family.

My youngest daughter was born with Cystic Fibrosis which claimed her life at age twenty-two. It had always been my hope to write a book about our lives with her, raising her and living day to day with the challenge of having a special person in our lives. I never managed to do it, however, until after she had passed. Even then it took me eleven years to accomplish. I just didn't have the courage to re-live those times until last year when I took place in a challenge to write fifty-thousand words in thirty days. I accomplished what I had always hoped to do; write a story to share with others who shared their lives with someone who needed a bit extra to achieve full potential.

# This Little Piggy
# By Sandra Rozanski

Living on the farm was just a way to inject abnormal thoughts into my mind when I was growing up way back then, long ago. I hardly remember it now but it has had the biggest bearing on my personality, more so than any other single thing in my life.

My family was not particularly spectacular, so to speak. Not on the average side either. As the middle child of three and a girl to boot, I had the odds against me from the beginning. Ragged on by my older brother, who was sixteen and treated like a second mother by my younger one who was five years under my age, I felt chafed between a rock and a hard place every waking moment that particular summer of the "Pig." Not an ideal place to be for a twelve year old girl. Still and all I had moments of dreaming of a Prince Charming one day who would sweep me off my feet and give me a family if not a castle or a glass slipper. Alas and woe is me, I was dead set that said "castle" would not be built on a farm.

Winters were dire in our neck of the woods so I really did not have much time for day-dreaming and in the summer the chores were just as rugged and kept the lot of us exhausted beyond human means. Up at five (my dad was up an hour earlier) and in bed by seven after the last slopping and animal feedings. We all barely had time to eat our supper and help my maw clean up the kitchen….my job while the boys helped dad to each their own.

Ricky, my older brother was nearly as tall as our pop and almost as strong so he took a lot of the load off of him, while "Ticker" fetched water and fed the chickens. His real name was Timothy but as a toddler he always made a weird clicking noise with his tongue so hence the nickname, which has stuck.

I always had to slop the hogs when Ricky was at some other chore. I hated it in the worst way with the worst passion. The grunting, snorting, smacking that went on was horrendous to my ears and anyone would believe those monsters never got fed, let alone twice a day. I hadn't even taken to them when they were newborn and halfway cute and I never minded eating the ham or bacon, not one whit. Ticker liked naming them sometimes and I took good pleasure in letting him know when we were feasting on so-and-so. Mean, I know but part of what would be the mold for my dark side.

Our mom worked as hard as two women, keeping up the small house what with the rough wood floors and walls. Cobwebs abound along with their weavers, sometimes fierce and nasty looking. Shooing out snakes of all sorts was also a given. Cooking meals for what seemed more like a family of twelve, rather than five over a fire in the hearth in an iron kettle took its toll as well. Our men ate with no shame for their appetites. And it was a bitter task to do the laundry by hand and then hang it to dry. Good weather was bad enough but in weather cold enough to drop your nose off your face it was always just too much. She was always straggled looking with her hair falling out of her bun, wisps floating around her pale cheeks dampened with sweat. I don't recall her smiling, not once. She'd got real sick and nearly died when she miscarried a baby girl in the fifth month. Tick was only two then and had no idea what was happening but I had an inkling since I remembered when mama was carrying him in her belly. She never did get back to the way she was before that happened and it took a long time for her to gain back any strength at all. If I knew anything for certain it was that I did not want this kind of life for myself.

When daddy decided to sell off some of the hogs that fall I was about as happy as I'd ever been, in fact could not wait. We kept enough for slaughter so as to have winter meat and the rest were gone when I got home from school the end of that day. Yippee-hooray, I went through the house singing and flopped down on my little cot against the attic eave. Ticker popped his head in the doorway which had no door and sat cross-legged at the end of the bed. He looked mighty solemn for such a young boy. I wondered what was going on but stayed silent. Finally he looked up from his hang dog position and I saw he was crying.

Oh, joy, I thought. He couldn't go to mamma because she was so stressed out that she would not have been able to help whatever it was bothering her youngest child. I knew she left a lot of the mothering to me. I didn't resent it....not really. But, it didn't leave me much room to feel like a kid myself. It wasn't Ticker's fault either.... I understood that which is why I just could not bring myself to be gruff with him when he needed me.

"Hey, buddy, what's going on?" I asked.

He chewed the bottom of his lip and let loose with a half dozen ticks before he got around to answering.

"Mason Foreman gave me a shove at school today and grabbed my sack lunch away. He robbed off my lucky copper penny too and told me that's how it's goin' to be every day from now on in until I die...." His lip quivered and the tears poured forth. I scrabbled him up to me and gave him a hug, squeezing until he sniffled and stopped crying

"You know, I think it might be a good thing for you to pop that little smart guy in the nose one of these fine days." His eyes widened in disbelief at the mention of that.

"He'll kill me sure if I ever try that," he stressed in amazement that I'd even consider the thought.

"Look, hon, what if I teach you how to knock out a few good punches, put a little respect into that infamous little demon from hell?" Ticker was well aware that I took no guff from even the toughest, biggest kids at school, boys or gals. He also knew I could not take down a scrappy bully who was also only ten years old, even if he was beating up on my little brother.

"Give me a little while to come up with a plan, okay?" He hugged me with a last sniffle and hopped off the bed to go do his chicken chores. I laid back and began to hatch a scheme to fix that little brat's wagon for once and all.

After supper that night and the dishwashing and kitchen cleaning I went out to make sure I had put away everything in the barn when I slopped the pigs. For the most part they were fairly quiet having more or less settled down for the night. The oldest hog was just standing there staring at me in the glow of the lamp I carried. He gave me the creeps. Penned off by himself away from the females he looked determined to have his way. I wasn't sure if dad was going to mate him up yet or if he'd decide to get rid of the rest of them and go to cows as he'd been talking lately. I sure hoped it would be the latter. I'd not mind milking a tiny bit as much as I hated slopping and cleaning out the hog pens. Ugh!!!

I looked right back into that nasty sucker's beady eyes and defied him to make anything out of it. It was at that moment it hit me just how to get even with Mason and I felt the grin spread out to my ear lobes. I latched the barn door and went back up to the house with a spring in my steps to go with that big grin on my face.

Next morning I was up as usual even though it was the weekend. The chores had to be done, no matter what, rain, shine, holidays, weekends, Sunday-go-to-meeting. It was all the same. I had no idea what it felt like to "sleep in." I still don't. It was something I never even tried embracing because I had to be moving constantly, busy with one thing or another in order to keep my mind from boiling over its thoughts.

I slopped those hogs with loving care, all six of them except for that big male chauvinist pig, pardon the sick pun. It was my plan to keep him hungry and away from the girls in order for my plan to work.

I got Tick his breakfast after I woke him up to get his morning chores done. Ricky had gone into town with dad to fetch supplies and mom was down with one of her "bad" headaches. We did not call them migraines back at that time. The use of the term was still new and not known to us country folk. They laid her low and sometimes kept her a-bed for days. I really had to take over all the work at those times. Usually it happened at least once a month. I pitied my mother to the core of my soul then and also re-enforced my choice to turn my back on farming life for good and all. I had started keeping a journal that year and found I had a touch of writing talent and really enjoyed putting the words on the paper. I never realized I had so much inside of me that I wanted to say. I never suspected I might get so good at it that I would become a known writer, published and thought highly of by some. I am thinking as I write this I have no intention of making it known to anyone. I will not submit it for reading because in fact it is truth. What happened that year of my twelfth birthday could still get me into deep trouble and while I never did find my prince charming nor have a family, I am with a charming chap from England and have been for most of my adult life. I would never want him to realize what I am capable of if I am backed into a corner or a dearly loved one should find him/herself in a world of hurt and need my help. I doubt he would stay around long after that came to light.

Tick was a different kid when he was not in school. He was more out-going and talked more and laughed a lot. He had a right to be that self every day and not be squelched down by a rotten young cur. Meek and easy going Tick was a follower then and now and always will be I'm sure. He did find his Cinderella and they married when he was twenty-three and she had just turned twenty-one. Annabelle was perfect for my younger brother and brought out nothing but the best in him and he was a great dad to their four kids. I doubt to this day that he ever told her of the bullying he suffered while he was still in single age digits. It was ever painful for him to recall. She would be horrified at my solution to the problem as well and a happy marriage would be right down the drain. But, I digress.

We finished our chores that weekend and I finished fine-honing my solution to Tick's problem. When we went back to school I took him with me walking along the way and explained what I had in mind. I kept my eyes open on him all day keeping myself in plain sight so that Mason would realize that I knew what was going on. It didn't completely keep him from torturing my brother but I think it helped a little. Tick never even minded leaving for school a lot earlier and kept himself in the boy's bathroom until the bell for his classes began. I waited for him after school so as to walk him home again. That went on for weeks as I slowly and deviously befriended young Mason and recruited him as a possible playmate for Tick. He never suspected a thing. The fact that he developed a major crush on me helped the most. We got to a point where he was sometimes walking home with us and watched as we did our chores before leaving and heading back home before dark. My mom surprised us by inviting him for supper on a couple of occasions. He still got in his punches on Tick when he could but I didn't rebuke his actions.

When the first snow fall came in early November it was really a doozy of snowstorms, drifting and pilling up against the sides of the house and barn, and burying the coop and the pigpen. Keeping them dug out was a real pain but again it was all part of farm life. We had to let them out at least part of the day and slopping was a challenge but they always ate greedily and wanted more. I had kept the male scantily fed making sure he was always feeling hungry.

Mason had come the weekend before Thanksgiving and stayed overnight with Tick and I heard them giggling all hours but also heard Tick cry out a few times in pain from the punches and pinches I knew he was getting from his buddy. It took all I had not to barge in and knock out his lights and beat the blood out of him to boot. I made sure when I got Tick up in the morning I woke Mason as well threatening him with no breakfast if he didn't come downstairs. Eating was his second love next to beating on my brother so he agreed.

I was out getting ready to slop the pigs when Tick wandered out with Mason behind him and headed to the coops. I called him over and asked him to help me carry the buckets of slop which he did with great joy and google eyes. I poured one bucket into the trough and they gals came running to get their fair share. Old boy was in the next pen and Mason carried the bucket over following after me like a puppy dog. I suggested he pour the slop into the trough and he juggled it up with him to the rail and leaned over to pour. He never even let out a yelp when I pushed him bucket and all into the pen with that four-hundred pound starving hog. He never even let out a peep when it began to feast on him with satisfied, loud grunts. Mason was gone in no more than ten minutes. Not even a trace of bone or blood or one hair on his head was left.

Tick came over and climbed up onto the fence where I was looking down into the pen and asked me what happened. He was not all too upset when I told him Mason had fallen into the pen and was eaten alive. Purely just an accident, I assured him with a wink.

Mom and dad were not happy about what happened to Mason but they bought the story. Mason's parents were not upset at all since they had no care for the boy. His pop had been beating on him since he could toddle and his maw never cooked a meal for him in his life, leaving him to fend for himself. He was an only child as well which suited them both just fine.

I only had to put a similar plan into action twice more. There was the time when a persistent suitor would not take no for an answer and I pushed him in front of a subway train. Five years after that I poisoned a co-worker who kept taking credit for my work. I got away with it both times. I have not had call for a long time to "wipe a slate clean" of a bothersome pest. No matter to me one way or the other.

Christmas Dreams Come True

By Tara Atkinson

Tara Darlene Atkinson was born in East Point (Atlanta), GA July 8th 1979. She graduated from Obion County Central High School (Troy, TN) in 1997. She has studied nursing, worked as a home health care provider, in nursing homes, and also in the natural health industry. Since childhood she has had a great passion for the genre of horror, in both print and film. She currently resides in Carrollton, GA.
https://www.facebook.com/tara.atkinson.31

# Christmas Dreams Come True
## By Tara Atkinson

Susan awoke confused, cold. She struggled to recognize her surroundings; an empty, concrete room, horizontal glass window on one wall, and one dimly lit light hanging loosely from the ceiling in the far right corner of the room. Her head was pounding and her vision was blurry at best. Breathing. She could hear herself breathing, slow and heavy to match her thoughts. Time to sit up and explore her surroundings. As Susan went to push her body away from the table she found that she was restrained at both wrists and ankles. As she began to struggle to free herself from what seemed like unnecessarily tight, leather straps there was a soft, yet maniacal laugh from the shadows followed by a growling voice, "Poor, poor Susan. All this time has passed and yet you still haven't learned."

"Who's there?!" Susan cried out frantically. The voice from the shadows laughed again,

"Go ahead Susan. Let's move it along quickly this time."

Susan's' tone was now hushed and baffled," Move what along?"

The shadowed voice spoke mockingly now, "I don't remember….this thing they said I did….It wasn't me I tell you, it wasn't me!" "Hahahaha," the voice become increasingly agitating and was obviously amused. "I killed the demon….there was no other way….Oh, Susan. You are a curious one."

"But..." Susan protested and before she could say another word the door to her concrete cell swung violently open and a large man dressed in hospital scrubs entered followed by a woman in a nurse's uniform. Both wore cold, grim expressions.

"Hold her down," the nurse said to the man. "She's quite a bit stronger than she may appear. Those restraints are rarely of little use. Susan began to scream and flail her body beneath the restraints as the man gripped her firmly.

The nurse stood over her holding a syringe, eyebrow raised in disgust, "Double dose this time child." Susan's body became limp, her vision once again blurred, and her fight beneath the restraints futile.

Dr. Marx was sitting at his desk reviewing Susan's file once more before what he hoped would be his final attempt at helping the young woman remember the brutal crime she had committed nine years earlier. Even more importantly, he hoped to get to the root of why she had committed such a crime. The police report was a bit vague: December 31st, 1960, 20 year old female found covered in blood, clothes torn, wandering barefoot on a bridge whispering repeatedly, "I killed the demon." Police retraced her steps back to the crime scene which was the home of her boyfriend who was found lying under a Christmas tree, throat sliced open and....A knock at the doctors' office door interrupted his reading, he closed the file, placed it in the desk drawer, took a deep breath, " Come in." His tone was authoritative, but not harsh.

"Here she is," said the orderly who was holding up a heavily sedated Susan from behind, supporting the full weight of her body.

"Sit her here," Dr. Marx motioned to the chair in front of his desk.

"Should I stay?" asked the orderly.

"No," replied the doctor smiling slightly. "I'll call should I need you." The orderly pauses hesitantly for a moment and then exits the office. Dr. Marx doesn't miss a beat," Lovely to see you again Susan." Susan, slumped sideways in the chair, glances slowly around the office,

"What is this?" she whispers.

Dr. Marx smiles brightly, "It's a celebration. I've decorated just for you, love." Susan then begins to examine her surroundings more carefully and notices the Christmas tree with multi colored lights, the snowmen on the desk, and as her gaze shifts upwards, the mistletoe hanging from the ceiling fan.

She then looked back at the doctor, eyes more alert now, smiling slightly, "A celebration. Yes. You love Christmas don't you darling?"

"Yes," Dr. Marx replied. "I do. Very much. Don't you?"

Susan stared at the Dr. coldly at first and then forced another smile, "No. Not particularly, but we've already been over this Christopher. For you, I will do my best to enjoy it. You deserve your celebration."

Dr. Marx smiled warmly and leaned forward in his chair, "And I adore you for that."

Susan, eyes still fixated on the Dr. lost her smile and said flatly, "I need a drink."

"Of course," the Dr. rose from his chair and made confident strides to a nearby table that had been converted into a min bar for the purpose of his session with Susan and poured two glasses of bourbon. He then turned to the record player that was sitting on the mini bar, set the needle, careful not to scratch the record, strolled back to Susan presenting her with the glass of bourbon, and extended his hand just as "Christmas Island" by Ella Fitzgerald filled the silence that had taken over the room. "Dance with me Susan." Susan turned up her glass and downed the bourbon quickly taking his hand.

"I can never complain about your taste in music Christopher," Susan said smiling as she allowed the Dr. to hold her close and nestled against his neck.

"Likewise, my love," the doctor spun Susan around and then pulled her back close to him again.

Her body was rigid now, "Please don't call me that, Christopher. I've told you it makes me uncomfortable."

"Susan," the Dr. stopped dancing now and held her face, searching her eyes for some indication as to what she may be thinking. "I only call you that because it's true that I love you and I do want to make all of your dreams come true." Susan's eyes went black and for the first time in his life Dr. Marx felt true fear. As if to confirm his fears, the hard right hook seemed to come out of nowhere and Susan threw him to the floor pounding his face with both fists and slamming his head hard against the thinly carpeted floor. Before the Dr. could even begin to defend himself the letter opener from his desk that must have been knocked to the floor during the blitz attack found its way deep into the side of his neck and then Susan collapsed beside him out of breath. Holding him, caressing his face, watching him bleed out, she whispered, "You can keep coming after me if you wish, but I will always win." The record began to play again and Susan lay smiling beside Dr. Marx's' now lifeless body and sang softly along with the song, " How'd you like to spend Christmas on Christmas Island......how'd you like to stay up late......you will never ever stray for every day your Christmas dreams come true...."

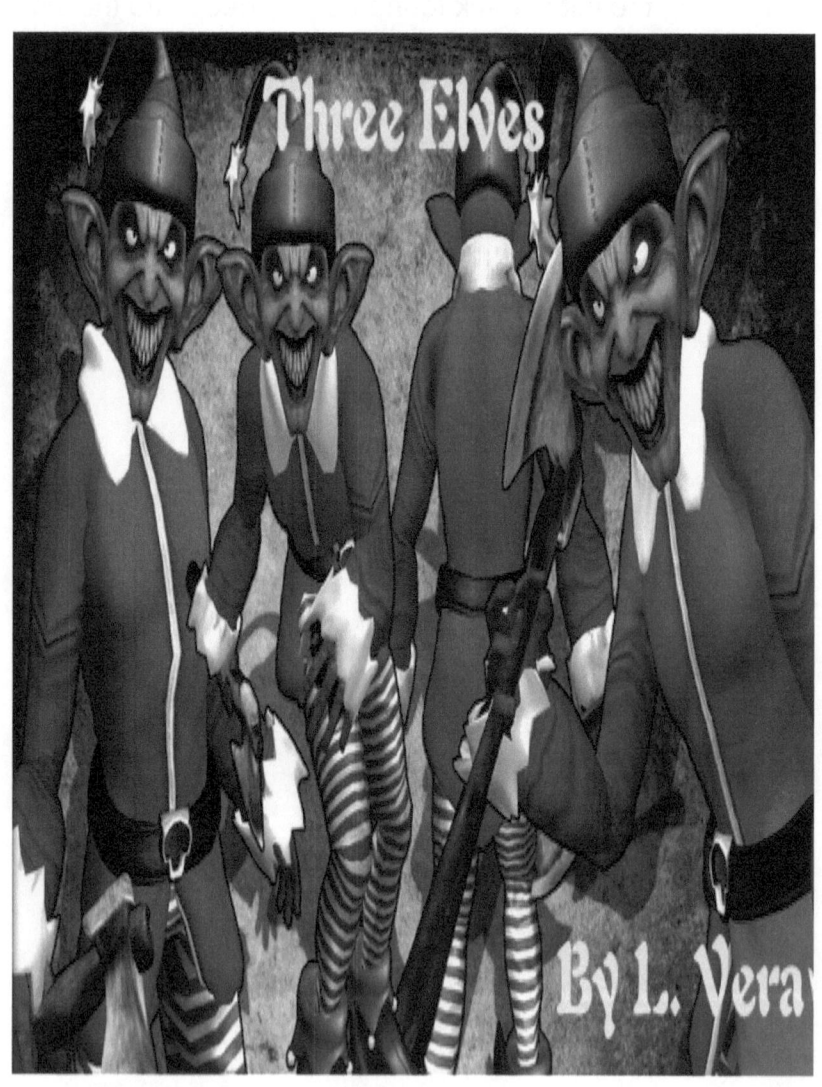

L. Vera has done many things like parkour, running away from cursed lamp posts, singing in a band, and killing people. Well . . . he kills people with ink, on his laptop. Ideas flow around him like a twister in a funhouse and I think it's safe to say his stories can be your friend on a dark stormy night. Don't worry he's harmless; it's his stories you have to watch out for.

Diary of a Madman was his first big thing, amassing four thousands readers. Along with some tiny contest wins he's been published twice with Good Guy Publishing, where two of his pieces have won first place spots in two separate contests and he runs the new Horror/Speculative Fiction/Crime Blog, AKAQ (www.AKnifeAndAQuill.com). Stop by and say hi. He replies to everyone, especially his fans.

# Three Elves
## By L. Vera

Three elves looked wide-eyed as their creation bobbled in place. They had built a friend out of body parts they had dug up from the local cemetery and had finally attached the last piece.

"Sweet!"

"Cool!"

"... Blah ..." The elf said with his tongue that hung over his lips and chin. His watermelon head had shifted to one side as he stared and poked at their new friend.

"I will bring him a toy," the older elf, who was lankier and more on the verge of malnutrition had said.

"I will bring him some food," said the elf with the large scar across his brow and cheek. He had crumbs scattered over his face and shirt. The stains had changed his shirt so that it no longer matched the others. It was dark red and always moist.

The last elf, who was not capable of many words, mumbled and shook his hands like he was casting an evil spell.

They left.

Alone, dead, dripping with blood plastered on its skin stood a human snowman. The darkness couldn't hide its grotesque features. It was a ball of meat shrouded with skin, stapled in some places and sewn in others.

The older elf was the first to return, his hands dripping with the red waters that once flowed through a young boy. In his clutches was a small metal car.

"Play!

He sat in front of the human snowman and pretended to share his toy, making it whiz and purr up and over their arms and legs until the second elf had returned.

This elf held a rotting sandwich that pulsated in squirming beats. He sat down where the other elf had sat and he snapped his sandwich in half and tried to feed it to his motionless friend; bugs fell, scattering away as they hit the floor.

"Eat!"

But the human snowman could not eat. There were no lips, just stretched skin over a featureless face. Crumbs fell to the floor but that didn't bother the elf. He simply scooped them up and gobbled them up seconds after they hit the floor.

The third elf had appeared with his gift. He hid it in his pocket and he approached the rotten pile of meat.

He stood inches from its smooth face and yelled, "Talk!"

Nothing came.

The other elves looked on, worried that their friend would destroy their new friend. And he insisted. "Talk!"

Nothing came but a large grunt and an even larger push that sent the body sliding against the floor.

The other two elves ran up to their friend only to find the surprise he hid shining through the evil they saw in his eyes. In his hand was a knife that nicked and pricked until they were defending themselves with their palms in desperation. Their eyes grew large as they felt the knife take away their life.

The maniacal elf stood over them slicing away at a piece of one of his friends. He carried the little sliver of flesh over to the human snowman and placed a pair of lips on its flat face. "There," the craziness had left his posture and voice, only calmness residing there, "now you can talk."

Christmas
Eve
By Yvonne Mason

Since learning to write at the age of five, Yvonne has wanted to be an author. She wrote her first novel Stan's Story beginning in 1974 and completed it in 2006. Publication seemed impossible as rejections grew to 10 years. Determined, she continued adding to the story until her dream came true in 2006.

Yvonne's brother Stan has been her inspiration and hero in every facet of her life. He was stricken with Encephalitis at the tender age of nine months. He has defied every roadblock placed in his way and has been the driving force in every one of her accomplishments. He is the one who taught her never to give up

# Christmas Eve
# By Yvonne Mason

The first time I saw him he took my breath away, actually took my breath away. I literally could not breathe.

Let me just back up and give you the back story as I lie here and ponder how I got here. I was a tourist in the city of Love at Christmas time. You know, Paris. Yeah, that city. I had been there for several days and had wandered the city enjoying all the tourist stuff, the Eiffel Tower, the Louvre, and all the lovely outdoor cafes. I was not there to find romance quite the opposite. I was there to heal a broken heart. At the time, it seemed like a good idea, now not so much.

I was sitting at an outdoor café drinking in the sights and enjoying a light lunch when he walked up. He was tall, dark and at the time drop dead handsome. His eyes were the color of black ink, his hair the color of coal, which showed off the sliver of white that ran from his widow's peak to the back of his head. His skin was a ghost white. His smile, well it was killer. He oozed charm and charisma almost to the point of nausea. My gut told me to get up and run as far and as fast as I could run. However, my body appeared to be glued to my chair.

He bowed at the waist and asked if he could join me.

"Mademoiselle, you have the look of a goddess. Why are you sitting here all alone on such a beautiful day?"

Taking my right hand he gently kissed it sending chills of what I thought was extreme pleasure down my spine. As he sat down in the chair across from me, a small voice nagged at my brain, "Get up and run." It said. However, I was helpless. My legs felt like they were paralyzed, my feet like they had been nailed into the concrete. I thought I was in the throes of a massive heart attack as I looked into those eyes. I do not remember what I ate or drank, those memories became fleeting the longer I sat across from him. In fact, I do not even remember his name. It must have been something exotic.

The afternoon sky turned into the night sky complete with thousands of twinkling stars that appeared to burn brighter than I had ever noticed before. The moon was in his glory. He shone full and round with a light that seemed to go on forever. I do not remember how I got from the café to this place wherever this place is. All I remembered was looking into those eyes. Those deep dark eyes.

So now, here I am in the unknown place, in this room filled with remnants of Christmas Past. The tree at one time must have been twelve feet tall, the branches now are bare and the ornaments old and brittle are the only thing, which adorn it. I see strands of tinsel, which at one time must have been silver but now is brown with age. As I looked around, I noticed the furniture was worn. It is not modern but more Victorian. It was then that I noticed I was lying on a fainting couch and my shoes were removed. I was not bound in any way but I found I had to struggle to sit up. There is a fire in the massive fireplace and candles burned in various holders creating strange dancing shadows on the walls. A chill was in the air, a feeling of anticipation and dread fill my soul, but I was not afraid.

I finally was able to struggle into a sitting position thinking, *"this is a dream, albeit a bad dream, but a dream nevertheless. I will wake up in my room, on my bed and under my covers."*

As I was contemplating how I managed to dream such a strange dream and how I was going to explain it to myself in the morning, he came into the room. By him, I mean the tall dark and handsome stranger who had invited himself to sit down at my table at the café.

"Ah, my dear, you are awake." He said as he sat down across from me in a wingback chair that had at one time been upholstered in deep purple, but now was more of a dingy black with what looked like moth eaten holes in various places where the stuffing was showing. On his lap lay what looked like a dress. Not just a dress but one from a different time period.

The look on my face must have spoken volumes because he smiled. The smile was not one of comfort or likability more of a sinister, dark brooding smile. It didn't quite reach his eyes. He had changed his attire. He was dressed more Victorian like the painting that my eyes were drawn to on the wall above the fireplace. I did a double take the portrait looked exactly like the man in front of me.

I looked at the painting, looked back at him and looked again at the painting. The voice from the chair said, "Yes, my dear, I am afraid it is me in that painting. It was painted a long time ago at Christmas time. It was a gift for my wife who tragically never got to see it. You see she disappeared on Christmas Eve. She had been out riding and as the hour grew later and night fell she did not return. Her horse did, but she was not found until months later. By then all that remained was her skeleton and the pieces of the clothing she had been wearing the night she disappeared. You look like her."

He pointed to a painting on the wall behind me, I felt a chill crawl down my spine, and I was looking at myself. I turned back to the man who had moved from the chair to stand in front of me. He had his hand held out. I took it without thinking. In his other hand was the dress; it was the same one in the portrait.

"Please tell me this is just a dream." I said in a small voice, the finger of fear piercing my heart.

"But my beautiful Lili, why would I want to do that." He replied. "You have come home to me after all this time. See, the Christmas Tree is waiting. Nothing has been changed all of us have waited for you to join us. Now be a good girl and put this on."

He handed me the dress which was moth eaten, and torn. I recoiled from its touch. He stared at me with those eyes, those hypnotic dark eyes. I could not resist. I took the dress and as if by magic it was on my body. I did not remember putting it there. It fit perfectly.

"Who has been waiting?" I asked as I tried to figure out how the dress had gotten from his hand to on my body. "Aren't we the only two here?"

His laughter startled me. It was as dark and foreboding as he was. "My beautiful wife, don't you remember? Both of our families had gathered along with all of our friends, we were going to announce that we were going to have a child, the first grandchild on both sides of the family. It was a time of great celebration. I was going to have a son to carry on the family name. But, you had to go riding. You said it would be the last time before you gave birth. You insisted that you had to go that day. I tried to talk you out of it but you would not hear of it. You killed my child."

The anger that spewed from his words took me aback. I wanted out of this twilight zone, I wanted back in my own room in my own bed in my own home. I started to run, but stopped dead still when I saw the others. Those faces came toward me, he was behind me. I don't remember what happened after that I passed out.

When I came to myself again, I was still dressed in the moth eaten gown, but I was in another room. It was just as grey, damp and dank as the first one. I was lying on a bed that was covered in a canopy that had seen better days. There were rips in the material and it hung in ghostly layers. There was no fire in the fireplace and the only light was a single candle sitting by the bed.

I had enough. It was time to find my way out of this house of horrors. Who was this man, who were these people? Why me? The most important question where was I? I didn't really care at this point how I got here I just wanted to get away.

Carefully and quietly, I got off the bed and walked toward the door. I noticed it was heavy and thick it looked like oak. I turned the knob and slowly opened it. Making my way down the long hallway to the stairs that looked like they might take me downstairs, I heard voices from below. They seemed to be having a full blown argument.

"What if she refuses to stay?" One voice, which sounded female, asked in an almost hysterical pitch.

"She won't refuse." Said the voice that I remembered all too well. I know it belonged to Tall, Dark and Gruesome. He never told me his name and I really was not interested in finding it out. I just wanted out the front door and off the property and back at my hotel so I could catch the first flight back to the States. So much for a nice quiet vacation.

"You know we are stuck here unless she agrees." This said by a third voice, a man's voice."

"She will agree." Said, Tall, Dark and Gruesome. "I know she will she has too."

What was I supposed to agree to? I had no clue. All I knew was I looked like that haunting portrait of the woman who I was supposed to be. I didn't know how that could be true because she had lived at least a hundred years before I had ever been thought of. The voices started again.

"Priscilla, you know her go talk to her. After all you are her mother."

I stopped dead in my tracks with my hand on the railing of the stairs. My mother? How did she get here? She had been dead for five years. Had I fallen into a different time warp? Was I going insane?

"Jason, she wouldn't listen to me as a child. That is why we are in the mess we are in now. You all know how strong willed she is. She will never agree."

That did it. I had enough. I was through playing with these looney tunes. I wanted to get to the bottom of this insanity and get on with my life. As I marched down the stairs and walked into what appeared to be a drawing room, several pairs of eyes turned to star at me.

Tall Dark and Gruesome smiled. Well, he didn't really smile he smirked. "Glad you felt well enough to join us the Christmas Eve." He said as he took my arm in his. "We were just talking about you."

"Okay, so this is how we are going to play it." I thought to myself as I pasted on a fake smile. "Well, two can play at this game."

Aloud I sweetly replied, "I don't know what came over me. I must apologize for putting all of you out. I just came into to say my goodbyes and I will be on my way. If you could just tell me where my purse and coat is I will not be a bother any longer. Oh, and Priscilla, for the record, I have no idea who you think I am, but your daughter I am not. My mother died five years ago and......"

I didn't get to finish the sentence, Priscilla said, "My dear, dear child, do you not remember the Red Rose you put in my hand that day. You said, "Mom, hold this until we meet again."

I looked at this woman like she had two heads. "Who told you that?"

"No one told me, my child, I was there in the casket. You wore that black lace dress. It was always too short, and you had the heart necklace around your neck that your father gave you for graduation. "

Before she could continue I said, "Stop! Just stop! I am not playing this game of charades and dress up. I am leaving."

Tall Dark and Gruesome held my arm just a bit too tightly. "Ah, my sweet wife, I don't think so. You see, in order for us to get past the Eve of Christmas, you have to agree to join us. You have to agree to join the child you murdered. You cannot leave this place."

A cold finger of dread slid down my spine. I must be mad. "Why do you keep talking about a child? I have never even been pregnant so how could I kill an unborn child on Christmas Eve?"

Tall Dark and Gruesome which I had shortened in my mind to TDG led me to a couch that looked like it might just collapse if I sat on it. He more or less pushed me down on the couch and walked toward a table. He picked up an old photo album and returned to my side.

The other gathered around as he sat beside me, giving me the creeps. "Forgive me for not introducing myself to you earlier. I would have thought that you would have remembered me. After all, we were very much in love. My name is Pierre LaBlanc. We had been married for six years and I had all but given up on children. But, then the impossible happened. You were pregnant."

As he spoke, he started turning pages in the dusty album. The odor of mold and mildew and something else I could not put my finger on caused me to cough and sneeze. TDG aka Pierre did not appear to notice. He just kept turning pages. The first photo was hard to see it had almost faded to nothingness; I could barely make out the fact that there was a man and a woman standing side by side and she looked like she was wearing a dress similar to the one I now wore.

"This was our Wedding day." He said as he gently touched the page.

The next photo was completely gone. He sighed as he passed over it and turned the page. "This was our honeymoon to Italy. I had never seen you happier."

I looked at the photo and the face I saw staring back at me looked anything but happy. In fact she looked sad and haunting.

"This is not me. I don't know who this woman is but it is not me." I said as I got up to leave. I had enough. "I am walking out the front door and that is the end of it."

There was laughter from all the faces in front of me. One man who I had not yet been introduced to said, "My dear, dear Child, it is Christmas Eve. I don't think you will be going anywhere. You see my dear, ever since that night we all have been stuck here at this time in this place ever since that night. We cannot leave and neither can you."

Heads nodded in unison.

"You people are all insane. I am leaving. I am walking out now."

I walked to the front door turned the handle and nothing happened. I tried again this time more aggressively and again nothing happened. I felt the eyes on my back. I turned and there they all stood waiting.

The woman who said she was my mother with a sadness in her voice said, "My sweet daughter, there is no way you can leave. You see you are also between worlds. Until you agree to stay, we cannot leave this place. We want to be with the baby, the one who left us way to soon. We can hear him crying but we can't reach him. You must stay. You must help us."

I looked from one to the other. I even looked at Tall, Dark and Gruesome. Something began to draw me to them. Maybe it was the crying of a baby. Maybe it was the idea that no matter what I did I was stuck in this place whatever this place was. Maybe I was just tired. After all I had just gotten out of a bad relationship, lost a child months earlier. Fled to Paris to re-group.

Wait, I had forgotten I had lost the baby right after he left me. He said he didn't want to be tied down. He said that he had not signed up for three o'clock feedings, baby sitters and smelly diapers. It hit me then like a ton of bricks. I remembered. The pain, the blood, the loss. I was alone it was Christmas Eve.

It couldn't be it didn't happen. The last thing I remember was being lifted on a gurney in a hospital, with people all around. There was a bright light overhead. Then the voice said, "We are losing her."

I heard it again, the crying of the baby. I found myself following the sound with a heart of love. I had to find it. I had to embrace my child. The others followed behind me. I walked straight to the nursery like I had been there many times. There he was in the cradle waiting for me.

Smiling, I bent over and picked up the blanket and cuddled the tiny bloody piece of human flesh or what was left of it. I heard sighs behind me and felt the soft breath of a slight wind. I looked behind me and they were gone.

Only my child and I remain in this house on Christmas Eve. I found the old rocking chair and sat down with my child. Softly I sang an old Christmas Carol to him while I watched the decorations on the small tree in his room move softly on the tree.

I had come home.

The Bad Shelf Elf

By G.J. Lentz

© ABC

G.J. Lentz lives, works, and writes in the American Midwest. He has had six short-stories of varying genre (fiction and non) published of his own and with other talented writers since 2011. He enjoys and explores writing in fantasy and science-fiction, as well as horror and paranormal. When not working and writing he enjoys swapping postcards with folks from all over the world, brewing beer and mead, and taking it easy with his faithful and furry feline companion, Oreo the Cat. You may follow his meanderings online at: https://www.facebook.com/gjlentz...

# The Bad Shelf Elf
## By G.J. Lentz

"Marissa!" the woman yelled with disbelief. "Oh, no you did not!" She stood in the door way and surveyed the chaos of her kitchen. She gave her daughter "the look", a little girl of seven who stood in the middle of the catastrophe with her little elf doll in her hand.

"It wasn't me, Momma," the child said with wide apologetic eyes: big, brown, sad, puppy dog eyes.

Jenna was unfazed by her daughter's claim of innocence, it wasn't the first time of late, and she knew- but hoped against hope, that it would be the last. The kitchen was completely destroyed: cupboards were opened and their contents strewn about the counter tops and floors, some broke open like the cereal, the rice, the sugar, and the flour...silverware, cooking utensils, pots and pans. The fridge was the worse: condiments were open and spilled inside and out, eggs broken, spilled milk. Her daughter stood before her with tears strolling down her eyes, and she was just as much a mess as the kitchen with smudges of chocolate syrup, pieces of cereal stuck to her strawberry hair, flour and sugar, and one could only guess what all else plastered the side of her face, and her clothes. In her hand she held the little elf doll, with its beady eyes and goofy grin. Mr. Elf, as the little girl had been calling it, was fairly dirty too, but that was the least of the woman's concerns at the moment.

From around the corner trudged Allen, Marissa's two year old brother. He wore only a diaper which sagged terribly. He had a look of complete glee about his face, his very messy face. Head to toe the boy was a walking menagerie of food stuff. He squished his little hands which were caked with a concoction, he grinned at seeing his mother, squishing up his now-not-so-cherub looking face and letting loose a squeal of pure delight. The mother groaned and sighed, Allen didn't know any better, of course.

"I guess this was all Allen's doing then?" She asked her daughter. "Or, maybe it was Mr. Elf again, like last time?" The girl had made a previous mess a few days before, having ransacked the home office of which she knew she wasn't ever to have any business being in. It hadn't been nearly the mess the kitchen was, and it hadn't been her fault then either.

The girl nodded that indeed it was Mr. Elf who had don't the deed. She held the doll out to her mother like she was handing over a captured criminal. "Honest and for real," Marissa whimpered.

"I don't have time for this Marissa, I really don't. A mess is one thing, lying is another, but this is unacceptable. Look at all the stuff that is wasted and has to be thrown away!" the mom said with practiced contained anger. "And your brother! He's filthy, and he could've been hurt, this was not safe at all. What were you thinking? Why would you do something like this? I don't understand where your head is these last few days, and its Christmas time! Baby Jesus and Santa are watching and they know Marissa, they know everything, and they know that you have been a very bad little girl."

Marissa's tears began to flow more readily and her lips trembled. "I'm sorry, I'm sorry, I'm sorry!" That was all she could say through the tears.

"I know you are, but sorry does not clean this mess up, and it does not make your bad choices go away. We have company coming and I have things that need to be done, but now I have to clean up your brother, and all of this," she scolded some more with a slightly tired and defeated tone to her voice. She snatched the doll out of the girl's hand and flung it to the corner. Mr. Elf took a swift aerial dive into the trash can.

Marissa watched and then she turned her head with a look of terror and shock which gave the mom cause to pause. "He's going to be very bad now; you flung him and threw him away…" her words trailed off with her disbelief and obvious concern for the elf doll.

The mom was taken back for a moment by the look on her daughter's face and then her words. That moment quickly passed as anger boiled back up. She was more shocked by the level of anger she felt, she made a fist and opened her hand repeatedly, and she realized she was clenching her jaw tightly. She had never been so furious in all her life, and it scared her. She took a couple of calming breathes and collected herself. She knew having an outburst would only exacerbate the situation, that's what she told all the other parents who were her clients, and she knew it to be true.

"I'm going to go clean your brother up," she finally said. "You're going to start throwing away all this spoiled food, understand? Dishes in the sink, food in the garbage, and when I am done with your brother I'll finish up while you get yourself cleaned up. This is the end of it for today, but we are going to have a very serious talk with your father tomorrow, understand?"

Marissa nodded and started cleaning up as she had been told, while her mother grabbed up her brother who had been silently amusing himself with the sticky and gooey mess all about him.

She grabbed him with outstretched arms to try and avoid as much of the mess transferring to her as possible. Little Allen giggled; it was all a game to him. Crossing the kitchen they passed the trash can and the boy squealed: "Ehhph! Ehhph!" It was his first words, to mom's dismay. He pointed to the can and unintentionally flung a gloopy line of gunk across the floor, which elicited riotous laughter from the little boy.

"Yes, Elf," she replied with a roll of her eyes. "The bad, bad elf."

"Well, what happened here?" Ted asked after he had entered the kitchen from the back door. He carried a sack which he placed on the counter.

His wife, Jenna, was just finishing cleaning out the mess of the fridge. Freshly cleaned containers took up a portion of the counter behind her. She rolled her eyes at his question and began to fill the fridge. "Your daughter," she said dryly.

"Oh-oh, I don't like the sound of this," he said as he opened the jar of olives and plopped one in his mouth. He took stock of the trash can filled with quite the mess. A tiny beady eyeball stared at him amid the trash. Ted took the elf doll out of the trash with two fingers, a messy glob of food stuff slid from it. "Why Mr. Elf, whatever did you do to be thrown out with the trash?"

"Not funny, not funny at all. You should have seen this place, it was ransacked, and Allen was in the middle of it. Cupboards dumped out, food bags and boxes broke open, the fridge was destroyed, it was awful. Mr. Elf got the blame, and I threw him away in my moment of blind anger."

"I'm sorry honey," Tad said with true sympathy, but he had that stupid curl to the corner of his mouth where he unconsciously fought a full-on grin. Normally it amused Jenna, but she wasn't amused then and there.

"I don't know if this is some phase, or what, but it's going to stop. She is in her room, grounded until dinner, and she was warned to be on her best behavior this evening, but that we would be revisiting all of this tomorrow."

"Alright, we will," he said as he shook more gunk from Mr. Elf. "Bad, bad luck to discard the Shelf Elf like that though, Bad mojo and all that." He took the doll to the sink and washed it off.

The Shelf Elf was a long slender thing with a canvass like body of green material; it had a red color cut like a poinsettia leaf, red cuffs on the wrist and elfish boots which ended in a tiny jingle bell. The head and neck was wooden, the face was both carved and painted, and shellacked over. The eyes were beady, it had a sharp little nose, pointy ears, and some curly hair carved out that hung out from a red and green hat the same material as the body.

The hat was slender, but long, it ended sharply with another one of those little jingle bells. Ted squeezed the doll and shook it of the rinse water. The elf jingled slightly.

"There, all better," Ted said. He stared at the elf for a moment; his wife paid him no mind. While washing it he had thought the elf had had a pouty look about its carved face, which was strange, because it was the naughty smirk that had drew him to the doll when he purchased it from the local good will shop. He thought it must have been some stuck food stuff, and rubbed the face again, and sure enough the pouty look was in fact a smirk, just as it should be.

"Really Ted," Jenna asked as she watched him pat-dry the Shelf Elf, Mr. Elf as Marissa named him. "I never even liked that damn thing; I don't know what you see in it or Marissa for that matter. I'd almost rather she had an invisible friend. Really, it creeps me the hell out." She was pouring a large glass of wine, a wine he had brought in with him. She poured him one too.

"Well, you got to put up the decorations as you like, every damn year," he replied with sneer to his voice. "I think I can have this one thing, don't you?"

Jenna stopped drinking and stared at her husband for a moment from behind the glass she held to her lips. It was characteristically unlike him to have such a tone. He could be a smart ass, for sure, but in twelve years of marriage had ever spoken to her, or the kids, or anybody to her knowledge, with such an ugly tone. "You, okay?" she asked, and she took another long swallow of her wine.

He winked at her and took a long swallow from his own glass. Without a word he took Mr. Elf to the sitting room and placed him on the mantle across from the Christmas tree. "Now stay put, and don't cause any more trouble Mister," Ted jokingly said to the Shelf Elf.

From the kitchen there was a shattering of glass which made Ted flinch. He looked across to his wife who held her wrist in her hand. She was bent over the sink, water running, and she was slightly moaning.

"Jenna, are you okay?" he asked with concern. "What happened?" He walked swiftly into the kitchen from the other room. She held her wrist under the water and it all ran red. "Let me see." She had a good gash on her wrist, but it wasn't serious.

"I don't know, it just happened," she said with a groan and a slight sob. "I guess I just slipped and slammed my hand down with the glass and I got cut; I don't know."

"It's not so bad, really, you don't need stitches," Ted told her as he helped her and tried to comfort her. "I'll get the kit and fix you up; it'll all be fine, okay? Just breathe. He left her holding her wrapped up wrist above her heart.

Jenna had tears rolling down her cheeks, she had a sudden sensation of just utter sadness, and she didn't know where it came from. She was a childhood psychiatrist, she was supposed to be good with the mind, with feelings and thoughts, but then and there she didn't even know her own.

She looked at the glass on the counter and the spilled wine, and the spilled blood. She knew just a bit more of a different angle and depth and she wouldn't split her artery right open. Ted was a vet, not a doctor, but she knew she was in good hands, but the thought of such a slash to her wrist, and the unexplained emotions she was having really disturbed her. She thought about the day, it had been a little trying what with the mess Marissa had made, and then her husbands' unnatural snip when she really needed him to be her rock. She had downed her glass of wine pretty quickly, and had refilled it. She tried to remember what and when she last ate, but she couldn't really recall.

She looked at the bottle and saw it was still two-thirds full, so even what she drank and as quickly as she did shouldn't have gone to her head so much as it must have. She turned her head and Mr. Elf was sitting on the mantle in the far room, his head cocked but looking right at her. Fear and anger boiled, and that didn't make her feel any better about herself, or the day as a whole. It was a doll, just a doll, she knew it wasn't responsible, but for some reason things in the house just hadn't been right since it was brought home several days back. She knew it was a ridiculous notion, but there it was non-the-less.

Ted came back in with the first-aid kit, bringing her out of her thought and back to the then and there in the kitchen. Her wrist hurt, and she wanted another glass of wine.

Ted fixed her up, and they shared a glass in silence for a few moments before Allen began to cry from his room down the hall. He had been laid down after his bath so that Jenna could clean up before company came over.

"I'll get him," Ted said with a smile, thinking of her wrist being so tender.

"No, I will. Go see Marissa," she said. "She hasn't spoken to me since I scolded her earlier. It'd do her good to see and talk to you. I'll be fine. Deborah and Lyle will be here with the kids shortly."

From the other room little Allen wailed, a cry far from that of his normal when he was just fussing for someone to come get him. Jenna went after him and Ted went down the other end of the hall to Marissa's room.

Jenna flipped the bottom light switch which turned on a soft light in the corner, rather than the bright over-head light. She saw something over the crib-bed, and she gasped in a sudden moment of panic. She had seen a dark form over the crib, or she had thought. As she collected herself, there was nothing, there was no one, as she had believed in that very moment, just Allen standing in his crib-bed. He was red faced from his sudden crying and wailing. He kept swiping his little left arm, like he was swatting away at a fly, or how he did when he wanted to let his sister (or anyone else for that matter) to know that he wanted his personal space. Jenna took a calming breath as she picked him up out of his bed.

"There, there, Momma's little man," she said in a soothing voice, comforting her son and herself. She was still somewhat edgy from the panicked moment she had had. It was so eerily surreal, but there still was nothing and no one else in the room with her and Allen as she walked around and turned this way and that, inspecting the room and using the motion to help calm the child. She hoped the rest of the evening would be better and relaxing with their friends coming over.

"Hey you guys!" Marissa welcomed with jubilee as she opened the front door with her mother right behind her.

"Hello Marissa, Merry Christmas!" the woman replied, who held a squirming bundle to her chest. Behind her was a man, her husband, and he held the hand of small boy Marissa's age. He waved with a big smile on his face, happy to see his friend.

"Invite them in Marissa, it is cold outside," Jenna said with a laugh.

"Oh, yea! Please, come in! And a Merry Christmas to you too!" Marissa said as she opened the door further and gave them room to enter.

Ted and little Allen were just down the foyer. "Hey guys, Merry Christmas!"

The man, Lyle, hugged Jenna and gave her kiss on the cheek; he then proceeded down the foyer to greet his friend Ted. "Go on, make yourself at home," he said to his son as he relinquished his hand. "Hey man, good to see you, Merry Christmas! Oh, look at this little guy, getting so big!"

"Oh yea, every day, more and more the handful as well now that we are full-on Terrible-Two!" Ted joked as he handed his child off to his longtime friend. "How's the baby?"

"Really well, thanks," Lyle said as he greeted and played around with Allen who giggled and squirmed in the man's hands. "Getting bigger everyday too, but she's such a good a little baby. Hardly fusses, sleeps all night, unlike the other one had, good Lord what a difference. As babies, night and day, I am telling you!"

Everyone chattered on about this, that and the other as they shed their coats and scarves. After the initial excitement wore off they settled to the dining room for a leisurely dinner of take-out Chinese, and a bottle of cheap Saki, a tradition from their college days, years before, where they had all met and their friendship had begun. The last year they had gathered at Deborah and Lyle's, and they had had take-out Mexican and margaritas. Each year they did so the night before Christmas Eve. After dinner the older kids went off to Marissa's room to play, while the grownups and the little kids made themselves comfortable in the family room by the fire, and surrounded by the décor of the season: the Christmas tree, the garlands, the cards that had been coming in from family and friends around the mantle, and, to Jenna's chagrin, but Lyle's delight, the Shelf Elf who sat upon the ledge of the mantle and observed the goings on from its vantage.

"Oh, hey, that's one of those one things isn't it?" Lyle laughed as he got up to inspect the doll closer. "Elf on a Shelf?"

"Shelf Elf, I guess," Ted replied. "Marissa has named him Mr. Elf."

"Ef?" Allen asked pointing at the mantle, and started to cry with his face all squished up like he did when he was not pleased at all about something.

Everyone shared a laugh at the boy's expense; it was one of those amusingly pitiful moments.

"His first word, if it can be called that," Jenna said with a roll of her eyes. "Yes, that's the elf. Bad, bad elf, huh?"

"Bad elf?" Deborah asked with a laugh. "I thought those things were supposed to be good luck.

"Anything but if you ask me. I think it's creepy. Marissa and her father are enamored with the thing, Allen and I have a different opinion don't we little man?" To which he just buried his face in his mom's shoulder. She tickled him, and soon he had forgotten all about being upset.

Lyle studied the Shelf Elf, as he accepted a newly poured drink from Ted. "Where'd you get it? It looks old, like vintage?"

"The local good will place across town," Ted replied. "I was dropping some stuff off at the outside bin and it was hanging out of the opening by its hand, and I couldn't resist. Brought him home. It was that or a puppy," he whispered.

"I'd almost rather it was the puppy," Jenna said dryly as she drained her glass.

"Everything good," Deborah asked, sensing some tension from Jenna's voice.

"Of course," Jenna said with a big smile. "Hey, let's get some music going, and I think it is present time!"

Marissa and her buddy Phillip came running from down the hall, "Presents?" they asked in unison, and everybody laughed.

Jenna grabbed a remote and clicked it, but instead of the classical Christmas music she had had ready, an ear-bleeding cacophony shrilled from the rooms surround sound speakers, and the power winked right out, leaving them all in pitch blackness with a hellish symphony of unnatural noise screaming at full volume. Jenna fumbled with the control as they were all deafened by the unnatural noises. Lyle dropped his glass, which shattered on the hardwood floor. Allen and the baby Fiona both wailed their extreme displeasure, as did Marissa and Philip adding their own screams of bloody murder.

Then, just as suddenly as it had gone off, the lights all came back on: the table lamps, the wall sconces, the myriad of colors from the Christmas tree. The terrible sounds from the CD player still continued, however, and nothing Jenna did with the remote worked, and the frustration of it was evident on her face. But, then too it finally stopped.

Ted stood on the other side of the room with the power cord in his hand. The awful noise had been defeated, but the two little children still cried from the shock of the terrible sounds that had suddenly assaulted their little ears. From the other room Marissa and Philip crept back in, to them it was all a game.

"Oh, Jenna, your bleeding, are you alright?" Lyle asked as he stepped over his shattered glass to check on her. She was bleeding from her bandaged wrist.

Marissa came into the room to see what all the fuss with her mother was about, with Philip close behind.

"You guys go back in Marissa's room and play," Ted said with a smile, to show there was nothing amiss. "We broke a glass, but everything is okay. We will have presents in a few minutes, okay?"

Philip looked to his parents for reassurance, they both smiled and nodded, Deborah waving him on. He and Marissa did as they were asked.

"I probably tore it open some fighting with the remote, my goodness, can you believe that noise? I'm so sorry; I don't know what happened to the CD player." Jenna said as she fought back tears. Lyle and Deborah shared a glance, as Ted came around the other side of the sofa to see how his wife was.

"Let's go get you re-bandaged in the other room. You two don't mind watching the little guy for a minute?" He asked his friends. "She has a jagged, but not very serious cut on her wrist from early, still very fresh, we'll back in a jiffy."

"Yea, yea, no, go on, sure thing," Lyle said. "I'll get the glass cleaned up, sorry about that!"

"Oh hell, it's not the first time today," Ted said as he led Jenna out the room.

"Ef?" Allen asked, pointing at the mantle. "Ef?" he repeated.

Deborah smiled at the boy as she continued to coddle her baby, who had settled down. She hadn't even looked to the mantle, to notice that the Shelf Elf was gone…

The hour was late. The house had quieted to the soothing sounds of some soft Christmas like melodies. The presents had been unwrapped and enjoyed. Little Allen was fast asleep on one end of the sectional sofa, Marissa and Philip sat side by side with a picture book, oblivious to the world around them. To their other side laid the baby

Fiona encamped with cushions. The parents shared a slow dance: Ted swayed with Deborah, as Jenna swooned with Lyle.

"Well, we should probably get going," Deborah said as the dancing had stopped with the music. "It's been a wonderful evening, as always.

"What is Mr. Elf doing up on the Christmas tree!" Marissa said out of the blue as she and Philip laughed about it.

Ted first looked at the mantle, where Mr. Shelf Elf had last been. Then to the tree, as Mr. Elf was not where he should have been. "What in the world?"

Jenna scowled and sighed, "Get it off there would you? What are you thinking?"

"I didn't put it up there," Ted said under his breath as he stood up on his tippy-toes to retrieve the doll. "How did you get up there, Mr. Elf?"

Deborah gave Lyle a look, to which he just shrugged his shoulders.

"Come on Philip, tell Marissa good-bye, Ted and Jenna good night, it's time to get on home now," Lyle said as he gathered his little girl in his arms.

"Thanks so much for coming, sorry for earlier, but hey it was interesting, right?" Jenna said.

"No worries, thanks for having us. We ought to get together for Easter, if you don't have anything set?" Deborah asked as she gathered their belongings.

"Oh, sure, that'd be great, of course!" Ted said as left Mr. Shelf Elf back up on the mantle where he belonged.

They all made their way to the foyer as they hugged, and kissed, and said their good-byes. The three of them: Jenna, Ted, and Marissa stood on the porch and saw their friends off, little Allen was still sound asleep on the couch.

They all went back inside as their friends drove down the road. Marissa was sent off to dress for bed, Jenna gathered Allen up to put to his own room, and Ted worked on straightening up the room. Not long thereafter Ted and Jenna relaxed in each other's arms in their bed.

"You alright?" Ted asked. "You seem tense."

"Yea, just a little out of sorts, not sure what really, just the holiday blues, I guess," she said as she yawned.

"Wrist feels alright?" He asked, gently stroking it as he gave her a kiss on her forehead.

"Mmhmm, it's fine," she said sleepily. The two laid together for some time in silence, and eventually they both began to doze off, until Allen started to fuss from the down the hall.

Jenna started to get up to check on him, but Ted placed an arm on her, stopping her. "Stay in bed, I'll get him." And he went off to check on his son. Jenna laid in the darkness with her eyes closed, listening to the muted voice of her husband as he spoke to their son. Soon he was calmed, and before she even knew it she too was asleep.

She thought she was dreaming, at first, she had that sensation of having been asleep a good long while, but it couldn't have been so long. There was a weight at the end of the bed, and then motion, and the sheets and the blanket were disturbed. She thought Ted probably was crawling into bed, trying to be quiet and gentle, as he had come back from Allen's room to find her sound asleep. She thought it was sweet. He was a good man. She felt his hand slowly slide up her leg, and then she knew she wasn't dreaming. She smiled and giggled as he advanced further, stopping at just the right place, and focusing just the right kind of attention that her surprised delight was pleasantly replaced with something else altogether...

Morning shown through the curtains of the bedroom, the shadows of night abated and so too did sleep as Jenna yawned, stretched and awoke. She bumped her wrist, which gave her a bit of a shock of pain. To her left she immediately realized that Ted was not in bed with her. Normally she was something of a light sleeper, always had been, and at first she was surprised that she hadn't felt him arise. "Ted?" No one answered.

She propped herself up on her good arm, and saw her panties on the other side of the bed, and then remembered Ted having "came back" to bed last night. Did she fall asleep during it? She wondered. It was a weird sensation…she didn't remember them finishing, or maybe she had had more to drink than she realized. She laughed to herself, and sat up, and then was startled. That damned Shelf Elf was sitting on the edge of the night stand, propped up against the lamp, staring at her. It looked pleased and smug, and Jenna was anything but pleased. Seeing it there set her off. She was pissed.

Jenna flung the covers off and grabbed a pair of sweat pants that were hanging on the chair. She quickly put them on and started for the doorway, but abruptly turned around and snatched Mr. Smug elf unceremoniously from the nightstand. She marched down the hall and around the corner into the living area, the kitchen was to the left beyond the dining room, no one else seemed to be up.

She intended to fling the Shelf-Elf but her wrist, her badly cut wrist suddenly flared with intense pain. It actually brought tears to her eyes. She dropped the doll, and stumbled back to the hall. "Ted?" she called out, meaning to have yelled for him, but all she could manage was a squeak. She made her way down the hall, the kids' bathroom lay between both Allen's room and Marissa's, and it was closer than going back to her own room, where she and Ted had their own. She was bleeding through her small bandage, and it hurt like all hell. Something wasn't right.

She passed in front of Allen's open door, and there was Ted. He was sound asleep in the rocking chair with Allen in his arms. Ted opened his eyes and smiled at her, at first, until he realized the anxiety in her eyes, and that she was holding her bloody wrist. His eyes widened and he stood up briskly, but careful to try and not disturb Allen. With a couple quick and sure strides he was leaning over the crib-bed and laying Allen down. He didn't wake.

"Jenna?" Ted asked as he stepped to his wife. "Geeze, what happened?"

"It hurts; *I don't know*, it hurts," she hissed through her clenched jaw.

"Alright, come on, let's go down the hall so we don't wake the kids," he said as he led her down to their room. They passed the entryway to the living and dining areas, Jenna glanced and gasped. "What? Is it your wrist? Maybe we should get you to the doctor," Ted said.

In their bathroom he sat her down on the toilet, she was trembling.

"My God, Jenna?" He asked as he held her hands in his to try and help calm her. He couldn't understand why she was so worked up, something just didn't add up. "What is going on? You need to talk to me, or I'm calling 911."

"*That fucking elf*," she whispered. "Why would you do that? Especially after last night…" she forced herself to say through her anxiety.

"What do you mean? The Shelf Elf? *Seriously*? What now? *What* about last night?" He really didn't understand what her negative obsession was with that doll. She was supposed to be a psychiatrist, and she couldn't even see how she was projecting onto a damned doll?

Jenna loosed a nervous laugh, releasing herself of some of the anxious energy that had been like a grip over her mentally and physically.

"You're mad because I never came back to bed? For god sake Jenna, I don't know what has gotten into you the last few days, but you're really starting to give me cause to be concerned. I guess I fell asleep in the chair with Allen, now what are you going on about?"

"I woke up this morning and you left that *damned* doll on the nightstand. First thing for me to see when I got up, and you know, *you know*, I've never liked it. And after how you came back to bed last night? You just can't leave well enough alone?"

"What?" he said incredulously. He didn't recall coming back to bed last night, and he certainly hadn't pranked her with that doll. Why would she think he came back to bed and what did she mean by *the way* he had come back to bed?

Just then Marissa started screaming from down the hall. Both parents forgot their own issues of the moment and raced out of the bathroom and their bedroom to see what was wrong. As they were passing the archway to their right the fireplace roared to life, seemingly all on its own. Ted slid to a stop, cursing out loud from the craziness of it all. Jenna stumbled into him, and almost tumbled down to the floor with sudden impact.

"What the hell?" he said under his breath as he stepped through the way to survey the living area. The fireplace came on at full blast, belching flame, but he couldn't see how it was possible. It wasn't a gas fireplace, and even if he hadn't put out the fire from the night before, it wouldn't be roaring now.

Marissa was down the hall screaming from behind her door unintelligibly. Jenna told him to go check the fireplace before the house burned to the ground, she would deal with Marissa.

Ted surveyed the living area and the fireplace. The fire seemed unnaturally hot and bright. He wondered if something had somehow gotten into it, or if something had been dumped from above maybe: a prank of some kind? He grabbed the poker and unlocked the grate. He poked at the fire, trying to keep his distance, it was damn hot. The fire just winked out. Ted was left standing there thinking how odd it was. He thought he saw a shadow; he started to turn before the Shelf Elf caught his eye. It was standing up on the mantle, actually standing- or was it propped? It sure looked like it was standing from where Ted stood, but its face...*Holy shit*, Ted thought as he met the doll face to face. Its face had a comical look of surprise about it: its eyes were wide with joyful surprise, and its mouth was open in a similar fashion of expression.

The fire roared back to life, flames singed his arms and he could feel the heat radiate over him like when you opened the oven. He stumbled backwards in surprise and defense, tripping over his own two feet, stumbling, stammering, until he crashed into the Christmas tree. He and the tree fell to the ground in a grand crash of broken branches, shattered ornaments, and crushed presents.

From down the hall Jenna couldn't hear what was going on with Ted. Marissa wouldn't stop wailing to even acknowledge her mother, and now Allen was awake and hollering bloody hell as well. Marissa's door was locked, which caused Jenna to start panicking. Her mind was racing. All she could do was squeezing the door knob and pound on the door with her other hand, the one with the bad wrist. Pain shot through her arm and hand with every contact, but she didn't care. She couldn't get the door open, and it hadn't had a lock, so how was that even possible? "Baby, open the door for Momma!" she yelled from her side.

From within she could hear her daughter's screams, screams that sounded like complete terror.

"Ted!" Jenna yelled down the hall. "Ted!" But Ted did not answer.

She ran down to the other part of the hall towards Allen's room. She side stepped to look into the living area, she didn't see Ted, but the fireplace had been put out. Allen screamed and wailed some more, at least his door *was* open. Jenna turned for Allen's room. She caught a glimpse of him standing up and hollering, looking so pitiful in his fit, which broke her heart- at the same time that she saw it, she realized what Allen was yelling in his fit: Ef. Ef! Ef! He repeated and sure enough there was the damned thing sitting in Allen's crib. Jenna cringed and raced for the doorway, but the door slammed shut right in her face, and Jenna slammed faced first into the door. She pounded both fists and tried the knob, but no luck. It was like Marissa's door, no lock but it wouldn't budge.

Jenna sank to her knees and crawled around the corner for the living area, it was all she could do. She crawled to the living room like a wounded dog. "Ted?" she called out.

She managed herself around the sofa and saw his feet and legs splayed out on the floor among the ruined tree and the discarded presents. "Ted?" she called out again. She reached his body and tugged on his pant leg. "Ted!" she yelled.

It took everything in her, but she stood, and she stood over the mess that was her husband entangled in the tree. His eyes were open, even his mouth was open, slightly so. He was still, so still. The kids were still screaming in the other rooms, but there wailing was soon drowned out by the thundering in her ears as her heart and mind raced. "Ted?" she croaked. But Ted wasn't answering. His eyes weren't even moving, or blinking. Jenna began to back step away, until she was in front of the fireplace. She turned her head and the Shelf Elf was staring at her, one eye frozen in a wink. She didn't understand how, she had seen the damn thing in Allen's room. And then she forgot herself and Ted, as she thought of her kids.

Before she could act, the fireplace roared to life again. Jenna's clothing and hair caught fire, and she stumbled backwards in fear, flailing all about. She ran into the side table which held Ted's brandy and rocks glasses. She and the bottle and glass went crashing to the floor, igniting a greater fire in the room…

Lyle and Deborah held the two children between them out in the cold and snow of Christmas Eve. Across the street their friends' house was a burned out shell. Allen and Marissa were spent of their tears. They had nothing left, and the two adults, parents themselves, wondered if the kids, particularly Marissa, even really and truly comprehended what had transpired that morning. They were both in shock and disbelief at the tragedy, they had just been there the evening before, and now their friends were gone, and they were left to pick up the pieces with their surviving kids.

The rescue responders had little information to offer: someone called 911 after seeing flames in the home through their own window next door. Several neighbors had come over to try the door, but no one could get in, someone had been on the other side of the house and could see the kids crying in their rooms through their bedroom windows. They broke the glass and rescued the kids as the fire raged on the other side of the house and smoke began to waft in under the kids' bedroom doors. Thank God for that, both Lyle and Deborah knew.

They were told they could leave, after the two of them had been confirmed as being in charge for the well-being of the kids in the stead of their parents. Lyle and Deborah were their god-parents, and legally assigned to take charge of the kids in such an event, as had been Jenna and Ted for their own children. They took the kids away from it all, Lyle holding Marissa, and Deborah holding Allen. They were putting the kids into their car, securing them in; the kids were unnaturally but understandably quiet. Lyle and Deborah spoke to them in hushed and empathetic tones, trying their hardest to not break down themselves. Every five minutes or so Allen would sniffle and snuffle with little gasps of breath and trembling of his lips, as if he was going to start having an episode, and rightly so, but he was being a tough little man. Marissa was silent and seemingly unemotional, but kids dealt in different ways. She made eye contact when spoken to, but she didn't offer much else in recognition or reciprocation. Lyle buckled her in the backseat next her brother, knocking something out of her hand accidently as he did so.

"No!" Marissa had yelled, startling both Lyle and Deborah who had just finished securing Allen's car seat.

"What is it darling, it's okay, it's all going to be okay," Lyle reassured her as he stretched down to the floor board for the object that the girl had lost. It was the Shelf Elf, and it had a very sad looking face. Lyle hadn't remembered that from the night before, he had remembered it had had a besmirched face. Maybe it was a different one, or he just had had it wrong. He picked it up and handed it back to Marissa. "See, it's alright, you have Mr. Elf, keep him safe now okay? You and Allen are coming home with Deb and I. Fiona and Philip are waiting with presents," he said to her with a forced smile. Marissa offered nothing in reply, but took the doll and held it close to her.

Down the road a ways Lyle and Deborah spoke in hushed tones to not wake the kids. They had fallen fast asleep. Lyle kept looking at the kids from the rear view mirror as he drove, which made Deborah nervous. "Watch the road, I got them," she had told him more than once, but he couldn't help himself. In truth, he kept looking at Marissa more than anything, and even more than that he kept looking at that doll of hers, the Shelf Elf. Every time he looked he swore to himself the thing was looking right at him, and with a different expression. He kept adjusting the mirror and stealing a glance.

"I swear if you don't stop it, we will pull over and I will drive Lyle," Deborah told him with finality.

Lyle adjusted the mirror and stole a look one more time, he was about to tell her alright, and in his mind he meant it, but when he looked again he saw the doll head spinning around slowly on its neck and it seemed to be laughing…

Deborah shot her arm out towards the wheel, startling Lyle and causing him to swerve the wheel. His focus came to the road ahead and his eyes grew big with shock, and he panicked just as Deborah yelled, "*LOOK OUT!*"

Marvin Anderson was born very early in his life and spent most of his formative years as a child. His love for storytelling and performance lead him to stand-up comedy, acting, and internet radio. Marvin has written several sketch and one-act stage shows in addition to performing stand-up and improv. He is the host of two internet radio shows, A Man's World (amansworldradio.net) and The Undercard (facebook.com/radioundercard). Marvin lives in the Detroit area with his wife and their fur-babies.

# Dirty Santa
## By Marvin Anderson

'Twas the night before Christmas and like every year
Santa started his mission with a six pack of beer.
He beer-bonged the first two and shotgunned two more
The last two he chugged then went out the door.
Eight reindeer were tied to the sleigh two by two,
On the back read a sticker, "It's called Christmas, Ya Jew."
Mrs. Claus said, "I hope you fall out of that sleigh,"
"And plunge to your death. That would just make my day."
"Eat shit you old bitch," slurred St. Nick with a start,
Then he climbed on the sled and released a loud fart.
"There's a kiss for you, darling," his stink, it did linger.
"Fuck off," she replied and gave him the finger.
Santa turned to the reindeer, he pulled on the reins,
Took a nip from his flask then called out their names.
Now Fuckface, now Asshole, now Cum Stain and Maggot
On Dildo, on Douchebag, on Dickhead and Frank.
We must fly through the night and I don't mean to be rude,
If this takes too long, you'll all be dog food.
They rose in the air and turned south in a hurry.
The snow they kicked up swirled and danced in a flurry.
They flew 'round the world bringing good kids some toys.
You see Santa loves children, especially boys.
The miles they flew took no time at all
And at each house he stopped, Santa had him a ball.

He'd leave a few presents then put his plan into action.

Raiding the fridge he left only a fraction.

He ate all the turkey and biscuits and rolls.

He drank all the whiskey and vodka and Stroh's.

By the end of the night Santa Claus was quite drunk

And the gifts that he left were really just junk.

A shoebox for Mary, an 8-track for Harry,

Broken iPod for Carry, a tampon for Larry.

At the last stop, he found his sack empty, 'twas shocking

So, Santa's solution was to shit in a stocking.

With the gifts given out and no food left for cookers,

Santa headed to Vegas and picked up some hookers.

He started with Cinnamon, Bambi, and Candy.

Then finished with Diamond, Ginger, and Brandi.

He did things to these girls that no gentlemen try.

Things that would make even R. Kelly cry.

When Santa was done he got back on the sleigh,

Tossed each girls a fifty then went on his way.

He arrived back at home just before noon.

Mrs. Claus said, "I hope you enjoyed all the poon."

"You're a dirty old bastard" she said with a sneer.

"I can't help it," said Santa, "I only cum once a year."

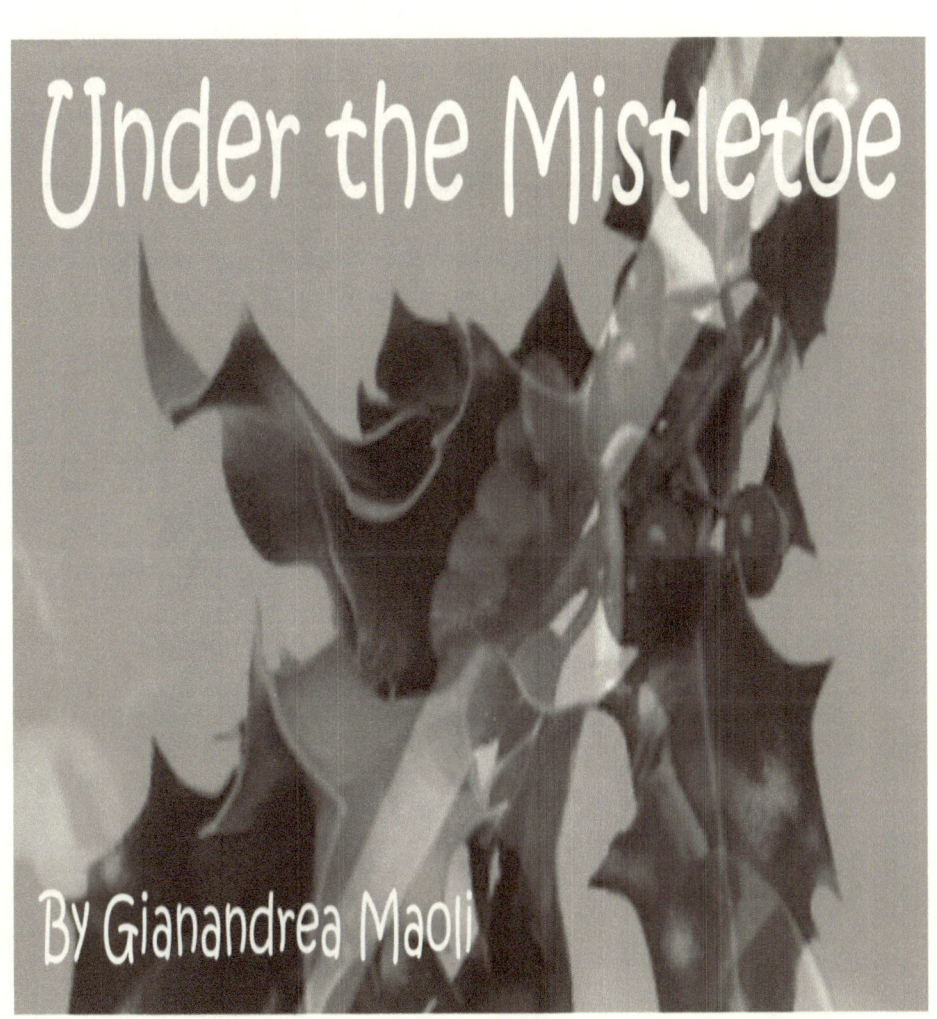

# Under the Mistletoe

## By Gianandrea Maoli

Gianandrea Maoli currently works at a tax prep firm providing project assistance for publishing tax returns and making files ready for e-filing. The job makes it easy for him to do many things he loveds including time for freelance writing,, which is something new that he is learning to explore. He minored in English with an emphasdis on writing exercises' and tecniques. He has also written various blogs on Facebook and have entered writing competitions with thr South Carolina Junior Chamber.

For the time being he has focused on writing short stories revolving around characters who have lost hope, yet find ways to overcome their challenges.

# Under the Mistletoe
# By Gianandrea Maoli

There the white bear stood growling with all paws outstretched. It stood over six feet tall and slashed wildly as if fighting off the pains of the winter snow. The creature lunged forward, but fell hard upon the powder covered terrain. Looking behind, it saw a metal creature clamped down upon its leg right above the foot. The bear stood up on his own paws and tried to move forward, but bellowed with a deafening roar as the jagged, razor sharp fangs of the metal monster buried itself deeper. Attached to a thick link of metal rings that made movement for the bear virtually impossible, its teeth shredded through the layers of skin and began to cut into the bone.

"Damn it, Carl! We need to put this bastard down now!" Said one man wearing a black heavy hooded coat with a large sled behind him. "Otherwise, he's going to pull on that trap so hard he'll rip his leg off just to get to us!"

"I get it, Joe, I get it!" Said another with a thick black beard. He was wearing the same kind of coat and holding a double barrel shotgun in his hand, "I'm just trying to get a clean kill shot. You know how tough these sons of bitches are."

"And if you don't take your shot now, that son of a bitch is going to kill us! Now shoot already!"

"When I get a good view of his chest, that's when I take it and not before! Otherwise, he'll have two wounds and get even more pissed! In short, I know what I'm doing, so shut the hell up!"

Joe huffed with annoyance while Carl walked closer to the bear, aiming his weapon towards the roaring wounded beast. As he did, he kicked snow into the bear's face, which just made it shake his head. He kicked it even more and the bear just began to roar and started to swipe towards him. The claws just barely missed Carl's gun, but the beast pulled harder on the chain. Onward Carl kicked, hoping to get the reaction he wanted.

*Stand on your hind legs, damn it! You know you're done, just quit making it worse!*

One more swift kick of the snow and the bear's boiling point reached its limit, standing up straight and raising both its claws, charging down upon the man below him.

*Done!* A shot rang, shells tearing holes into the bear's hide right below the chest and exiting through its back. Blood rained down upon the powdered terrain and turned the crisp white surface into a crimson red.

The bear staggered for a few moments and gave one final gruff before falling face first on to the ground. The face was buried into the snow and the roaring beast gave no more breath or sound. Carl walked up to it slowly and prodded it with his gun. Seeing no movement, he motioned to Joe.

"Let's load him up now...he's not going to do anything." Joe nodded and brought the sled over by the bear. He uncoiled the rope that was lying on the sled and tossed it over the side. He bent down and grabbed the underside by its shoulders while Carl laid down his gun and grabbed it by the back end. They picked it up and started moving it over the sled.

As the men worked on loading the bear, above them out of their eyesight sat a young boy with long silver hair and blue eyes. He could not have been older than 10. He held an icicle which seemed to glisten like a prism. He wore a gray cloak that appeared to be tied by green mistletoe. He gave no smile, but simply stared hard and long.

"You, who the hell are you?! You here to report us?!" Joe moved his gun up towards the trees above.

Carl, who was working on tying down the bear, looked at Joe with puzzlement. He looked behind him and saw nothing in the trees except for bare branches, swinging wildly in the brutal wind.

"Joe, what's the deal? Who are you yelling at?"

"Well, I saw...he was...ummm..." Joe looked furiously around, but didn't see anyone there. The trees were empty and simply moved with the wind. He was sure he saw a boy there…

"Nothing, forget it. Let's just get going."

Carl shrugged and finished making the final ties on the sled, then went over to the front with Joe and grabbed two more pieces of rope that were tied to the front. They grabbed one strand a piece and pulled and walked slowly, carrying their prized white silent creature behind them.

Out of their sight, the small boy appeared again standing by a tree, twisting and turning about his prism icicle. With a sinister smile and his subtle childlike laugh, a flurry of snowflakes whisked by him and covered him up completely.

The flurry then moved forward in the wind, leaving nothing behind but small footprints of where the boy once stood.

"That's a pretty fine catch there, men. Where did you spot it?" A man in a thick brown hooded coat stood next to the bear examining its teeth and claws while Carl stood over and watched.

The three men were standing in a wooden shed laden with hay. It was lit by a lantern hanging on the ceiling. There were also several large freezer boxes along the walls, and hanging over each of them was the head of an animal. One of them was a wolf. Another a deer. Another a raccoon.

Carl, who was now sporting a green turtle neck and thick ski pants, focused his attention on the man examining the bear. Meanwhile, Joe, now down to a sweater and jeans, was leaning on one of the containers, yawning and occasionally looking at his surroundings.

"Found it in the woods about 15 miles from here. It got caught in one of our traps."

"Well, I'm pretty surprised," remarked the vendor. He then moved over the bear's body, pushing up against the skin and occasionally stroking the fur. "The hide's pretty thick and so is the fur. I just never seen a bear like this before."

"Neither have we. We actually thought it was a polar bear at first."

"I can see why," the vendor stood up with his arms crossed and looked down at the silent mass, shaking his head in disbelief. "I mean, the fur is just as white and it's pretty big, but...the face is just so different. It looks more like a grizzly than a polar bear. Something else really odd about it too..."

"What do you mean?"

"Well, I don't know, maybe I'm just imagining something, but...while I was examining the face, I thought I saw a tear."

Joe, feeling a little anxious and interested at this discovery, stood up and walked over to the sled to accompany the men.

Joe kneeled down and looked closely at the eyes, which were both shut. He looked around anxiously to see if there was any sign of a stream that may have run down the cheek or perhaps some other sign of a teardrop. Standing up, he gave a loud gruff and looked at the vendor with annoyance.

"Come on, really?! First off, last I checked, bears don't cry! I know it! I've watched plenty of documentaries about them on National Geographic and YouTube!"

"Has anyone ever told you that you tend to sound a lot less like a dumbass when you're not talking?" Sneered Carl as he looked at Joe.

"Screw you! Fine, you're smart, I'm dumb! Happy, jackass?!" Joe then looked back at the vendor while giving Carl the finger behind his back. Carl simply snickered at the sight.

"In any case, the bear's dead! So how could he be crying or do anything at all?"

"Look," the vendor replied with a tone of annoyance. "I said I may have just imagined it, alright? No need to get snippy with me! All I'm saying is that the whole thing is odd, tear or no tear! You just don't find an animal that looks like this around here."

"And that's a fair point," Carl said as he put a hand on Joe who was about to say something else. Joe then stood back and shook his head while Carl continued. "I imagine the meat is still valuable though, right?"

"Oh absolutely! I can even offer you extra for the fur! It's a rare coat indeed!"

"Meat sale alone will do just fine, thanks. Christmas is just a couple days away from now, so I'd like hurry on and I'd like to get something really nice for my two daughters at home."

"Sure, sure, I understand. I'll head over to my house real quick and get the check. We'll then settle up and you two can be on your way."

"That will be fine, we'll wait for you here," said Carl as he offered his hand and the vendor took it to shake it. The vendor then walked through the double doors and closed it behind him.

As he walked outside, he tightened the jacket around him, trying his best to block out the bitter cold. Snow and wind blinded his view, but just a few feet away he could see his cottage home. As he took a few steps, he stopped momentarily as he thought he heard extra foot steps behind him. He turned around and called out, but there was no answer nor did he see anyone there. Thinking his imagination was getting the best of him again, he continued his walk. He had just stepped onto the front porch and placed his hand on the knob, but felt his body freeze in place.

He tried so hard to scream, but he couldn't. All he could muster was a subtle gurgle through his throat as blood ran from his mouth down his lips and dripped onto the porch. He looked down in horror and agony at the sight of his torso being covered with ice....as well as the sharp end of an icicle puncturing his throat.

Joe leaned back on one of the coolers again, tapping his foot on the ground. He looked down at his digital watch and gave a gruff as he looked at the double doors. Carl sat by the bear, just looking at it with interest, not paying attention to Joe's impatient demeanor.

"The hell is taking him so damn long!" Joe yelled as he banged his fist down on the freezer. "We have to walk back out in this cold crap! I'd like to avoid having to do that in the middle of the night!"

Carl said nothing, but leaned close to the bear and stroked its head. Feeling annoyed, Joe continued on, hoping to get Carl's attention.

"I can't understand why this guy has to have all these animal heads over each of these box freezers," said Joe as he looked at the head above him, which displayed a raccoon. "I mean, just put a sign over each freezer to tell customers what kind of meat it is! I don't know, maybe the guy is trying to be unique, but if you ask me it's damn creepy!"

Still silent, Carl looked closely at the eyes, trying to see if he could catch a glimpse of the tear drops the vendor spoke to him about earlier that evening. There was no sign of any such thing nor was there any sign of movement at all. He gave a heavy sigh and leaned back, looking up and down the body in wonder.

"Hello?? You think you can actually pretend to give a damn, Carl?" Carl turned towards Joe to see him with his arms crossed and with an angry look on his face. Carl stood up and shook his head.

"Joe, look sorry, okay. These past few years haven't been easy for me, you know."

"Look, I get that. That's why we came out here in the first place. Now your trade is paying off for a change."

"Only because I have fewer mouths at home to feed, Joe," Carl said with a low somber tone.

"Look, these things happen, alright. Just deal with it. You're doing what you need to do and you're doing it for the ones that need it the most, alright? So stop it with the self-pity bullshit already. Now how about we focus on getting our asses out of here and find out what's keeping the guy out so long.  We've been here for 15 minutes already and the guy's house is right outside!"

"Alright, alright, enough already! I'll go check on him and see what's going on. I just hope he's okay."

"We're out here in the middle of a blizzard and you're wondering if the guy is okay! Well unlike him, we don't have a house just outside of here to keep out the cold!"

"Yeah, I know.  You've done nothing but complain about it for the past 15 minutes.  I'll go check on him now...if anything it will help me get away from your constant whining."

Carl then turned and walked towards the door while shaking his head.  He grabbed his coat near the door and then opens the shed as he walked outside.  He could hear the sneering from Joe behind him as he closed the doors.

"Jackass."

Carl walked out to the house that lay in front of him. It was barely visible in the fury of the blizzard but he knew from the faint outline that it was near.  He carefully placed his steps, trying to find the same foot prints left behind by the vendor so as to not to fall deep into the snow.  However, the storm was so furious that the prints were beginning to fill up fast.

As he focused his sight, he could see the image of a man standing on the porch.  Carl quickened his pace a little and began to call out.

"Hey, are you okay over there?  We've been waiting for quite some time for you in the shed.  Is everything alright?"

The figure stood motionless.  Carl walked onward and inched closer to the man.  He was merely inches away when he set foot on the porch and placed a hand on the vendor's shoulder.

He pulled away suddenly, feeling the bitter cold travel up from his fingers through his arm and all the way down to his spine.  Carl held his gloved hands close to his chest.

*What the hell? My gloves are thicker than that bear's hide! How could I have felt that? More importantly, what in the world is wrong with this guy?*

Carl walked around to the vendor's face and became even more horrified. From top to bottom, the man was covered in ice. Carl could clearly see his bodily features, clothing, and face, but the layer of ice that wrapped around him made the vendor look like a life-like statue. The expression on the vendor's face was even more disturbing: his mouth wide open with wide eyes as if he was screaming in agony.

Carl also looked at the man's throat as something protruding from it caught his attention. A small point was sticking out of it. It was crimson red. Carl gently ran his finger over the point, which cut through the glove fingertip like a knife and nearly made contact with his skin.

Fearing the worst, Carl ran back to the shed, shouting out Joe's name.

Slamming the door behind him and throwing down his coat, Carl looked around frantically and continued to shout.

"Joe!! Damn it Joe, where are you??? The guy is dead! He's dead and a block of ice now! There's some crazy shit going on here! We have to get out of here now! The money's not worth it! Let's just get out of here! Joe, answer me, damn it!"

Louder and louder was Carl's voice and frantically he continued to look...until he stopped to look at the box freezer where Joe once stood. Running down the sides were small streams of blood, which appeared to be frozen in place. Swallowing hard, Carl moved quickly over to the freezer.

"Dear God, please don't let it be so," whispered Carl as he slowly opened the chest. He stepped back in horror as he saw frozen limbs and a torso, lying on top of what appeared to be animal meat wrapped in plastic. The inner walls were painted in red blood.

Suddenly, Joe heard the sounds of dripping from above, colliding upon the decimated body parts in the box. He followed the drips with his eyes up along the wall and found something mounted in place of the raccoon head.

It was Joe's head, pinned up against the wall in place with a frozen look of terror. His entire head was covered in ice save for the opening under his neck, which was dripping blood that ran down the severed spine still attached to it.

"So good to know it got your attention." Carl turned to find the boy in the gray cloak, standing next to the bear and tossing his icicle. He smiled as Carl stared at him.

Carl, flaring with anger, ran to the boy and grabbed him by the cloak, lifting him off his feet. The boy continued to smile as Carl looked at him with rage.

"You little sick bastard! You did this?! What's wrong with you?! These people have done nothing to harm you!"

"On the contrary, they did enough...just like you have. And now, you're not going to do it to me anymore...ever again!!!" The boy raised the icicle and jammed it down Carl's chest just above his heart, which caused Carl to fall down on his knees and scream in pain. The icicle punctured the chest and its point shot through his back, covered in blood and splattering it upon the hay covered floor.

As he grasped his shoulder, he felt a cold and painful shiver there. He looked to see it being covered slowly with ice and growing downward along his arm. It then spread outward to his other shoulder and then moved down his torso and arm, which eventually covered his legs.

Carl remained there, frozen in place with his hand still covering the punctured shoulder. Only his face remained warm and free from the cold prison. He looked at the boy who stood grinning and still holding the icicle in his hand.

He slowly twisted it loose, cutting up the flesh of Carl even more which resulted in Carl crying and shouting louder with pain. The icicle was now out, dripping with

Page | 141

blood from Carl's wound with even more blood slowly pouring out in small streams down his chest.

The frozen chest made it very difficult for Carl to breathe, much less talk. Still he had to know what was going on...and what he could do to get out of this situation, so he spoke with a weakened tone.

"Who...the hell are you? What do you want...with me?"

"Awwww, now really, you really don't recognized me? I mean, I know it's been a long time since we've seen each other. But still," the boy leaned down and placed his finger under Carl's chin, tilting it up to make eye contact. "I'm sure your memory is still decent....even if you decided not to care about me anymore."

Carl looked closely at the boy. Nothing really stuck out for him as far as what the boy looked like. He appeared very pale and his silver hair was nothing like Carl had ever seen before. Then he looked again at his eyes, which seemed like the only normal thing about the boy's physical appearance....his sky blue eyes.

And then Carl remembered those eyes belonging to a young boy from years ago. A boy Carl imagined sitting on his lap while the two of them were riding down a sleigh together. They speed so quickly that rest of the forest was lost in a blur. As they came down the hill and slowed down, Carl looked up and saw a woman in a white coat with bright blue eyes....

*Those eyes....my love...my heart...*

"Billy...is that...you? But...how...after these years? You're still alive...and haven't aged a day....yet except for your eyes you look...different..."

"So glad you paid attention to my eyes, father. It was the only thing physically I didn't want to have changed. I wanted you to remember me....to remind you of what you did to her...to us!"

"Ana...my love...oh my love..."

"Don't talk about mother like that!" Billy leaned down again and pulled hard on Carl's beard. "She doesn't deserve to be told lies of your love only to be deceived again! She even came for me when you wouldn't! You were going to leave me to die!"

"3 years ago...that day...I remember...you were out in the snow very late..."

"Yes. That was my fault I know....I just loved the snow....loved playing in it all day and night. I could never get enough of it. So I went out with my cloak and played. I went too far into the woods on my own and got lost. The storm was harsh....just as it is tonight."

"Ana...my love...she went looking for you...couldn't stop her..."

"Ahh, so you didn't want her to find me then?" Billy released the grip on Carl's beard and stood up. He walked around Carl slowly as he continued to speak. "You wanted me to die? Like you said, one less mouth to feed with the 2 other children you have?"

"No...not like that....I begged for Ana to wait...while I called the rangers....I didn't want to lose you both."

"Fair enough...but she went anyway. She came looking for me while you slept."

"Ye....yes," Carl's voice became weaker as he recalled the tale and he looked down with streams of tears running down his face. "I...awoke....looked around...she was...gone...went with rangers next day...couldn't find....spent so many weeks...."

"Oh how sweet...you spent all those weeks looking for us," Billy said sarcastically and leaned down next to the bear. He turned to look at it. "Then you realized you had better priorities. You're hunting career. You sure couldn't let any more chances of getting good meat for a profit, could you?"

"Not like that....I had family to feed...was alone...2 baby girls..."

"And what will happen to them if they wander off? Are you going to stop hunting if you ever lose them too?" Billy gave Carl a hard stare with a sneer look on his face.

Carl said nothing, but continued to stare down to the ground with tears continuing to stream down his face.

Billy shook his head and looked at the bear. He patted it gently on the head.

"When I got lost, I stumbled upon this icicle," Billy said as he held it loosely in his hand. Carl lifted his head and focused his sight on it. "I don't know where it came from, but at the time I found it I was frozen nearly to death. I was starving and freezing and then I touched it and the power of it surged through me. It's given me some incredible powers...as well as wondrous miracles...even for mother." Billy leaned his head upon the bear's and continued to stroke the head.

"By that time, I was wandering around the woods, experimenting with it and figuring out what I could do with it. Then all of the sudden I found Mom. She was lying face down in the snow. I still remember shaking her so hard. I tried waking her up...even shouting out to her...but she was already gone. Then..." Billy looked hard at the icicle and turned it around as if captivated by its glittering shine. "Somehow, I was able to preserve her spirit in this. Although her body was gone, her spirit was still alive. I wanted to keep her alive in this winter cold until I could find our home again...so I placed her spirit into this bear. I stayed with her and we tried to find our way...but neither one of us could remember how to get back home...nor did we ever see you. The more time passed, the more I hated you for leaving us alone. And then today, I saw you and that man....killing her!"

Billy moved quickly over to Carl and grabbed his ears. He pulled them hard and Carl yelled in pain as he felt the cartilage slowly crack and tear under Billy's grip.

"You killed her...for meat and money! Well you had your way...happy now?!"

"I...didn't know it was her...." Carl's teeth gnashed together as Billy's grip tightened even more on his ears, cracking them so loudly that they sounded like glass grinding under someone's shoe. "I...would never kill her...I loved her! And I did try to look....but I have...my little girls to feed..."

"Right, you do..." Billy released his grip and walked back to the bear. "Until one day, you'll lose them too...and they will end up just like mother and I did."

"No...won't happen...I promise..."

"You're right, it won't," Billy said with a serious tone as he pointed the icicle towards the fallen bear. A bright light shined from it and the bear slowly began to move and stand on its legs. It looked around and it seemed to have a somber look on its face.

Carl looked closely and noticed tears streaming down the bear's face. His eyes widened as began to recall the vendor commenting about the tears.

*Could she have been alive all this time? Has Ana come back to me?*

*'Yes darling, I am back. And I love you still.'*

Carl looked around frantically. He heard her voice, but had no idea where it was coming from. Billy laughed and took a few steps back away from Ana and Carl, leaving the two of them to face each other.

"She's speaking to your mind, father. And she doesn't even realize what she is. I made sure of that because the reality of her condition would break her heart. She thinks she is still your Ana. Her love for you never died. In fact, when I brought her back, she cried the moment she saw this."

Billy reached for the mistletoe that was hitched on his cloak and placed it on his palm. Suddenly, it floated in the air right above Ana and Carl.

*'Oh darling, look, the mistletoe,'* Ana gleefully spoke into Carl's mind as she looked up. *'Do you remember? Our first kiss ever just before we got married...all those Christmas memories we had since...this was always my favorite.'*

"My God..." Carl said loudly as he realized what was about to happen as Ana was walking towards him. Her face was closer to his. "Billy...please stop this! You...said I hurt her and you by abandoning you both...that I didn't care! But look...at what you're doing! You're...using her for revenge...how is that caring about her? How...are you different from me?!"

Billy remained silent and smiled. He crossed his arms and simply stared.

"Billy, I get it now! It's....that icicle! It's changed you....making you do this! You have to...get rid of it! Otherwise, one day, you'll do the same things to your sisters! Please...stop..." Carl turned to Ana, who was now just inches from his face.

"Ana, wake up....fight this! Stop this! This...isn't like before! You're not...Ana anymore! You're not human....STOP, ANA!!!!"

'Merry Christmas, my love' spoke Ana gently into Carl's mind and her mouth completely covered up Carl's jaw.

Ana's lips moved passionately. She bit into him hard with her fangs. Which ripped into his cheeks, spilling a great deal of blood onto the floor. Several of Carl's teeth fell out as well. Then, a severed tongue dropped, covered in blood and ripped along the edges by Ana's fangs. Carl's eyes rolled back and his head went limp as it rocked backwards.

Billy walked slowly up to Carl's body, which was still frozen in place. The jaw was ripped and hanging off one side of his face with blood oozing and dripping onto the ground.

Billy climbed on Ana's back and patted her on the head.

"Come now, Mother, let's get cleaned up! Christmas is only a couple of days away and we don't want my sisters to be celebrating it without us, do we?"

'No sweetie, of course not. Let's hurry home! They can help us bake your father's favorite Christmas cookies when we get back home tonight.'

Billy smiled and held out his hand as the mistletoe floated back to it. He refastened it to his cloak and looked back at the icicle in his other hand. A smile came upon his face as he stared at it, singing to himself as they were walking out of the shed:

*Ho ho the mistletoe*
*Hung where you can see*
*Somebody waits for you*
*Kiss her once for me!*

ORNAMENT

BY RICK POWELL

Rick Powell lives in Oak Forest, Illinois with his son, Brad. He has been a lover of horror his whole life. He once got lost in the woods near Bachelor's Grove when he was 2 years old and has been lost in the woods ever since. His favorite authors include Lovecraft, Poe, Chambers, Bloch, Campbell, Ligotti, Machen and too many more to mention. He started out writing poetry and is currently working on his 4th short story.

# Ornament
## By Rick Powell

She is looking out through the kitchen window as the snowflakes fall gently from the afternoon sky. The small flower pots outside on the deck, their contents long ago dead, already have an inch of the winter's dust that has been collecting since early morning. She looks at the digital clock on the microwave on the white marble counter and starts to rapidly stir the wooden spoon in the plastic bowl of batter that she holds in the crook of her arm. *Damn,* she thinks, *I better watch the time with this batch of cornbread. I cannot believe I burnt that first batch.*

The cordless phone on the wall starts ringing and she looks at it with a frown. She pushes the button to answer it and tilts her head to hold it against her shoulder so she can have her hands free to continue the stirring.

"Hello," she says, as she blows a loose strand of blond hair out of her face as she stirs.

"Hi, Judith, It's Miriam. First snow of the season. I am so excited! This is going to be the best winter ever!" The voice squeals on the other end.

"Yeah, I know," Judith says, with a weak grin. She looks around the kitchen while still stirring. *The pot-roast! I have to throw that in now!* She thinks. "What's up?" She says, hurriedly.

"Just wondering if you are still going to make it to the craft meeting tonight. Agnes said that there will be a surprise for all of us. I can't wait! Oh, don't forget Tabby's crochet needles. She says those are her lucky ones and she has a new project for her parents this holiday." Miriam says.

"I have it all ready in my bag. I have the books, too. I remember how Agnes got upset. I don't want that to happen again." Judith says. She puts the bowl of mixed batter on the counter and wipes her hands on her gingham apron. She goes to turn on the oven and opens the fridge to get the pan of prepared pot roast out and sets it on the counter. She looks at the clock again. "Is there anything else I should remember, Miriam?" She says, as she lets out a sigh.

"Nope. Just try to not be so nervous. We all know you are new to the club. You shouldn't fret so, dear. Remember, the main thing is to have fun! That's what the holidays are all about." Miriam says. "Just feed that hubby of yours and make it as soon as you can. We all know how it is. We've been there."

"Thanks, Miriam" Judith says with a relieved sigh. "I just wish John wouldn't fuss about it so."

"Don't worry about him," Miriam says, with a giggle. "You'll put him in his place soon enough. He has been saying he will be more supportive. This is your time now. You need your girl time."

"Yeah, your right. Listen, I gotta finish up here. I'll just see you later, ok?" Judith says, as she reaches up and opens the cabinet to get the baking pan.

"No problem, Sweetie. Talk to you soon. Kisses!" Miriam says.

Judith hangs up and starts scraping the contents into the pan. She puts it in the oven that has been pre-heated and sets the timer. She looks out the kitchen window at the snow that is starting to fall more heavily. She has always loved winter. She remembers the times with her grandmother when she used to wake up and look outside. A blanket of white as far as the eye can see. Fresh. Serene. Unblemished.

*Yes,* she thinks with a sigh, *this is my time now.*

John pulls his BMW over the snow encrusted driveway when dusk approaches and pushes the button on the automatic door opener from inside the car and pulls into the 2 car garage. *Goddamn snow,* he thinks, as he slowly pulls in next to Judith's Nissan. *I hate the fucking winter. As soon as I make partner at this law firm, we are moving outta this fucking town. Warmer climes and the secretaries are better looking.*

He slams the car door, and walks into the adjacent door going into the kitchen as the garage door slowly closes, he shivers as the last of the winter breeze stops blowing in as the door holds back the freezing chill as it touches down. He walks in to the large kitchen, loosens his silk tie and sets his briefcase on the spacious counter island, the many hanging pots and pans glittering from the track lighting above.

"Judith, I'm home!" He shouts. He sees the red and green kitchen towels and pot holders on the oven and fridge doors and the small assorted ornaments hanging from the kitchen counter knobs.

*Jesus, you kidding me,* he thinks. "Judith!" He shouts. He walks through the kitchen and enters the adjacent living room where he sees the large mahogany table with a candelabra of lighted candles. The recessed lighting in the ceiling above is dimmed and giving the room a romantic glow. The lace place mats have the finest china and the silverware is glittering in the lamplight next to wine glasses as a bottle of Cabernet sits at the place setting near his end of the table, as if welcoming him. In the center there is a steaming pot roast with an assortment of vegetables in white china dishes surrounding it. Judith is sitting in the chair across from it with her chin in her clasped hands, wearing an elegant black evening dress.

"What's all this?" He says with a confused frown.

"Hello, dear. Welcome home. I just thought I would be spontaneous. How was your day?" She says with a smile and her eyes gleam from the candlelight.

He pulls out a chair and sits down quickly. "Shitty," he says. "Goldberg fucked up the MacMannus case and the whole firm is in an uproar. After 4 months, we have to do the whole thing from scratch again. Expect me to be late a lot. Damn, that smells good!" He says, as the aroma goes through the air. He starts to get the bottle to pour the wine. Judith quickly rises from her seat and grabs it. "Here honey, let me." she says. She pours the wine as her looks up at her.

"Well, I can get used to this," he says, with a smirk. "Did I forget an anniversary or birthday?"

"No, silly. It is the first snow of the season and I just figured I would get it off to a good start. We had a rough year and I want to make this holiday extra special." She says, as she starts to cut up the post roast and scoops some vegetables on his plate.

"Yeah, I saw what you did in the kitchen. I hope you aren't going to decorate the whole house like that, it'll cost a fortune." he says, with a slight grimace as he gets his fork and knife and starts cutting into his dinner. She walks to her chair with the bottle of wine, pours herself a glass and sits down with a sigh. *A simple 'thank you' would be nice,* she thinks.

"I thought you would like the kitchen," she says as she starts to fill her plate. "Agnes and the ladies gave me the idea. Miriam had a Feng Shui phase months ago and thought we all should do it as a group. Make the holidays a little more festive. When I see the girls tonight..."

The silverware clinks into the plate as John drops his hands down before the forkful of meat reaches his mouth. He looks at her with a glare. "That's why the surprise dinner. You're seeing those Harpies tonight. I knew something was up."

Judith looks to the side as she slouches down. She reaches for the glass of wine and brings it, shakily, to her lips. *Please don't yell,* she thinks. *Please. Let this be a good winter. A good season.* She takes a long sip and clears her throat and takes a deep breath. "John, don't be upset." She says.

"Why shouldn't I be upset," He says. "You are always off to see those bitches. Them, with their new- age nonsense bullshit and goofy ideas. All you talk about is them, them, them. They had you running around all September and October with their fall festival shindigs. All those crazy crafts you made for those damn kids. You spent hundreds on that crap."

She looks down, avoiding his gaze as she starts nervously cutting into the meat. "Dear, it was for a children's hospital. Most of those poor children have been in that cancer ward for years. Please don't be so insensitive."

"I'm not insensitive. Hell, the firm works with charities all the time. It doesn't mean that I spend all my time making trinkets and shit that no one has any use for. I give at the office all the time, for Christ's sake." He says, irritatingly as he starts eating.

*I know how you give at the office,* she thinks as she sighs deeply. *Dammit, Judith, don't think that way.*

She takes another mouthful of wine and looks at him. *After 8 years of marriage it has come to this.* "John," She says, as she straightens up and looks at him. "Tabby and her staff work hard at those wards. Those children need all the support they can get. If it wasn't for Tabby helping take care of me when I was in the hospital, I would have never met Agnes and the others. They helped me in so many ways. I feel good when I get together with them, like I am contributing and feel like I serve a purpose."

John wipes his mouth with the cloth napkin that was in his lap and throws it on the half eaten plate. "So, what you are saying is that I don't make you feel like you serve a purpose, is that it?" He says, angrily.

Judith puts her hands on the edge of the table and her shoulders slump. "No," she says, as she closes her eyes. "That is not what I meant. It's just that you are always at work and it does me good when I feel like I am contributing to something. We never go out anymore. All of our old friends have lives and families of their own now. This house is big and I just..." She pauses as she looks at him, her watering eyes, glowing in the candlelight.

John pushes his chair away, the legs making an irritating scratching noise on the hardwood floor and plants his palms on the table as he stands and glares at her. "This 'big' house was what you always wanted. I give you everything and still you complain. Fine! Go have fun with your little 'club' of bitches. I'm going out for a drink!" He walks away from the table and goes towards the kitchen.

Judith watches him go, frozen in her chair. "John! John! Don't be like this! Please!" She shouts, as she hears the door going from the kitchen into the garage slam shut. She looks at the table of food and the candles and puts her face in her hands and tries to fight back the tears as she thinks about her last words to him before he left, about other people's lives and other people's families. She silently sobs as the candle flames flicker, vainly trying to keep the darkness at bay.

***

Judith is walking up the snow covered brick walkway to Agnes' large house. The stones are illuminated with large lamp posts that light the way to the two story French country style house which is decorated with multitudinous colored lights and a rustic country theme, complete with large green garland accenting the gabled roof. The large oak door is practically covered with a giant wreathe with a soothing 'Welcome' sash across the face of it. She gets a comforting feeling as she slowly walks ahead looking in awe at the house. It helps dissipate the sadness from the argument she had with John hours before. She walks up the door and presses the doorbell with one gloved hand while trying to hold the large denim bag of crochet needles, yarns and books in the other.

The door opens wide and she feels the warm air from inside the spacious house. A tall, robust woman of about sixty years old looks at her and smiles. Her face, which seems years younger, is framed by curly locks of white hair and she looks in surprise at the denim bag.

"Judith, darling! You remembered! Tabitha will be so pleased. Here let me help you. We were worried you would not make it." She says in a gracious voice as she takes the bag from her. Agnes turns and almost flows away from the doorway, her floral gown, glowing as she enters the hallway to the large living room which is casting a comforting glow from a blazing fireplace. Judith closes the door behind her and takes off her snow-encrusted shoes and leaves them on the mat near the door, blending in with the other dripping shoes of various shapes and sizes. Her face starts to warm up as she enters the living room, three pairs of glowing eyes welcome her as the ladies greet her in pleasant voices.

"Judith, would you like some tea?" Agnes says, as she hands the bag to a petite middle-aged woman who is sitting on a leather love seat. The woman sets down a china cup on the coffee table with a grin, her lips the same shade of red as her shoulder-length hair.

"Judith, thank you!" She says. "I knew you wouldn't forget. These were my great-grandmothers. I feel naked without them. I hope they worked well for you." She takes out the needles and gives the bag back to Agnes. Tabitha then proceeds to take a half-finished Afghan and skein of yarn out of the large bag next to her and starts to crochet.

"I see you brought my books. Are you finished with them or..." Agnes says as she looks in the bag.

"I just have a few questions later, if you don't mind. Some of the instructions for my final craft are hard to understand." Judith says. "I would like to keep them longer, if that is alright."

"Of course, dear. Take all the time you need" Agnes says, as she looks at her with a smile.

"It took me forever when she first lent me those books," A thin black woman in a gold dress says as she sits in front of the fireplace. "I drove my late husband crazy all those nights reading through it. He was never a very patient man and never understood why a woman would get so involved in her hobby." She rubs her forehead and adjusts the headband that is the same shade as her dress.

"Well, men are like that, Fiona. We have to put up with all the 'boy toys' but the one time we have a little something we call our own, they get all whiney and pissy." A large woman with a deep voice says. She is sitting in a long, leather couch on the other side of the room. "My third husband, Harold, was that way." She shakes her head with a disappointed look on her face as her horn-rimmed glasses as focused on the needle point she is doing in her lap.

"That was your second husband, Gladys." Agnes says, as she pours herself some tea from the china set on the large coffee table. "You say the same mistake every time."

Tabitha giggles and shakes her head, her hands clacking at a frantic pace as she crochets. "I hope hubby wasn't angry you were meeting up with us tonight." She says, not even looking up as she knits.

"He...will understand in time, I hope." Judith says, silently. She sits down in an armchair near the fire, hoping the warm glow will not show evidence of her red eyes from crying before she arrived. Agnes gives her a sideways glance as she pours her a cup of tea and hands it to her.

"He will, Judith dear. After all, you need this after the year you had. He owes you your time. Getting out to socialize helps clear your mind. Men never understand what we women go through. They never will. You are new to our little group but remember, creating and crafts does more than ease our minds, it eases our souls, too. No therapist, religion or drug can ever make you feel like the feeling you get creating something with your own two hands." Agnes says as she stands before Judith, looking down at her with a motherly grin. Her eyes, flicking from the flames from the fireplace.

"Hear, hear!" Gladys shouts. All the other ladies chuckle, the sound reverberating around the room. The sound puts Judith's mind at ease as she smiles and sips her tea.

"So, Agnes, what is this surprise you said you would have for us?" A middle aged, petite blond woman says as she enters the room. In Miriam's hands is a large, silver platter with bite-size sandwiches on it. "I told Judith on the phone before that you had exciting news. I'm sure I am as anxious as everyone here to know what it is." She sets it down on the coffee table and moves next to Tabitha, giving Judith a wink as she sits down.

"Well, ladies," She says, as she stands before the fireplace in front of them, her hands clasped in front of her, "I had an idea to make this season a little special for all of us. You know that I am a strong believer in creativity. My family has a history going back generations on what to do to make the winter special in many sorts of ways. So many people believe in giving so I am going to give something to all of you."

"We will have a contest." Agnes says, as she looks around the room. The women look to her and at each other with puzzled, surprised expressions. They are all quiet.

"This is no ordinary contest ladies, oh no. You will have to put your minds to work. You will take one specific room in your house and decorate it to the fullest and most lavish extent possible. I am not saying going out and spending an enormous amount of money. Besides, I would have you all beat in that area, my dears." She says with a slight chuckle, the ladies around her mirroring her sound with their laughter.

"This contest calls for simplicity. Use your imagination. Use what is readily available to you. I want this to be a stress-free contest. We are doing this for fun, for each other. It will all be judged by using the old 'name in the hat' technique." She says, as she looks into their interested faces.

"Enough about that, what's the damn prize?" Gladys shouts out. The other women look at her and laugh.

Agnes smiles and unclasps her hand and raises her finger. "Funny you should mention that," she says with a wink. She turns around and gets a small, wooden box from the mantle. Its red-wood, polished finish glows in the firelight. "The heirloom in this box has been in my family for over 200 years. I will give this special piece of my family to the winner of our choosing. I am not going to open it until the lucky lady is announced."

The gasps and sounds of awe from all the women bring a blush to the face of Agnes. Fiona places her hands over her heart with shock. "Agnes, that is extremely generous of you! How can you even part with something so personal?" she says, wide-eyed.

"Ladies, we all know what are little group means to us. We all know the hard times we all have been through. We have all shared our deepest secrets and personal adversities," she says, as she looks at Judith with a tinge of sorrow. Judith looks down for a moment. "We are sisters. We take care of our own just like the sisters and mothers in my family have taken care of each other. I am not getting any younger and whatever I have learned through the years, I share with you. It is just my way of giving back to you all." She looks around the room with a look of pride and love.

"This will be so much fun!" Miriam says, excitedly. "I already have ideas."

"Just be sure to keep it to yourself, dear." Agnes says as she puts the box back on the mantle. "I want this to be just for us. We have all been doing projects throughout the years for our personal charities and functions and such that I think since we all know what this season means to us personally, that this should just be our own personal project. Judith," she says, as she turns to her, "I know you have been in our group for a short time, I would like to speak to you in a moment about a few things. I know you have some questions with those books. I am sure the other ladies will not have a problem with that."

The woman all agree. Miriam gets up and goes to Judith's chair. She places her hands on her shoulders and whispers in her ear, "This will be so much fun! I cannot wait to see what you create." She proceeds to go to the table and grabs a sandwich as Agnes says, "Well, ladies. If you will excuse me, Judith, can you come into the kitchen with me? Bring those books. You ladies can work on some of your crafts and I'll be right back." Agnes starts to walk down the hardwood floor of the hallway as Judith gets up and follows her, feeling slightly tense as she walks behind her, the books held to her chest like a nervous schoolgirl. Agnes' form seems to almost glide down the hallway. Expensive picture frames of various ancestors seem to watch Judith as she follows. They enter a large, luxurious kitchen, complete with copper sink and granite counter tops and a massive double oven. Agnes pulls out a chair at the matching kitchen island and motions Judith to sit. Judith sits; placing the books gently on the island and Agnes sees the tenseness in Judith's face and gives a comforting smile. She takes Judith's hand in hers and says, "Dear, I wanted to talk to you personally. I can tell something was the matter right when you came in. It's John again, isn't it?" She says softly.

Judith just looks at her and with a tear going down her embarrassed cheek, she proceeds to explain of the nights events leading up to when she first arrived, every few moments Agnes would pull a tissue out of the box on the counter and hand it to her, sympathetically, while listening intently to every word. The relief is evident in Judith's face as she bares her soul to the older woman and when she is finished, Agnes puts her arm around her shoulder. "Judith, we are here for you. It was meant to be that you were to meet us. It is your Destiny. Ever since Tabitha introduced you to me when you were in the hospital, I knew you would be a member of our 'little family'. We have helped you heal emotionally and physically and we will keep on helping you. Always remember that. You have come a long way in such short of time and I believe this project for this 'contest' will be a pivotal turning point in your final healing. Let us look at those books and I will answer as many questions as you have. I believe when you leave here tonight, you will have the confidence and strength to take the next step."

Judith gives her a smile and hugs the older woman. This time the tears that fall from her eyes are tears of joy and she says to the woman as she hugs her tight, "Thank you! Thank you so much. I can never repay what you have done for me. I love you, Agnes"

Agnes pats Judith on the back, lovingly, like a mother. "I love you, too, dear. No thanks are needed. Now, let's just go through those books. I'm sure the other girls will be fine. They have Gladys to entertain them." she says, with a slight laugh. Judith laughs with her as she dries her eyes and starts to open the faded cover of the first book.

***

The afternoon is chilly days later and while her husband was at work, Judith opens the front door to two large, parka clad men as they lug in the rope-bound Fir Christmas tree, trying to carry it carefully through the house. They tread slowly while their snow-encrusted boots slip slightly on the hard-wood floor as they carry it to the dining room. After they have set it in its large tree stand near the window, Judith claps her hands in mild excitement as they unbound the ropes and finish getting it in place. The 9 foot tree almost brushes against the ceiling and she looks at it with wonder, thinking the whole time the ideas she has to decorate it.

After she gives the men the generous tip and they leave happily, she proceeds to mop the floor and gets the things she needs to start decorating the room. She goes down to the spacious, unfinished basement and carries up the dusty, cold, large plastic totes that are labeled 'XMAS' one at a time and sets them on the floor surrounding the tree. She then starts to unload the contents of tangled lights, assorted garland and many glass and plastic ornaments wrapped in wrinkled tissue and goes through each item one by one with a slight smile and pleasant memories of seasons gone by. She comes across an ornament of an ivory cherub and her face becomes a small frown. She wraps it back up in the tissue and puts it at the bottom of the tote. *Get those thoughts out of your head,*

*Judith,* she thinks. *This will be a good season. That is in the past.*

Hours later, after putting up the loops of green garland around the ceiling, the placement of the candles on the mantle by the fireplace and cleaning up, she looks at the white lights of the tree as it reflects off the night-darkened bay windows. The red, patchwork tree skirt gives the high, bottom space of the tree an eerie glow. Judith looks with a sense of accomplishment. She disregarded the ornaments and knows the only way she can finish it is with John's help. This is something we should do together, she thinks. She brushes her hands off on her jeans as she hears the door in the kitchen from the garage open to the grumbled cry of John.

"I'm home!" He bellows.

"In here, Honey!" She answers, with a contained tinge of joy in her voice. After a few moments, she hears him enter while she is still gazing at the tree, she replies, "What do you think?"

"I could see it as I was pulling in," he mutters. "What's for dinner?"

Her eyes open in shock and she turns to him with a slight gasp. "I'm sorry. Oh my gosh, I totally forgot. Maybe we can order take out. The creative mood just hit me, dear. I'm sorry." She goes up to him and puts her head on his shoulder and her arm around his waist and leads him to the tree, the lights reflecting in her proud eyes. "Isn't it lovely? Maybe after we eat, we can finish decorating it. It will be just like old times. Remember? Like when we first got married? That old apartment on the north side of the city. We spent hours on that little place and it was cold and cramped but it was still beautiful when we finished." She says as she looks at him.

"Yeah, but I'm starving and tired. Let's just eat first. Maybe we can do it tomorrow." He says, as he turns coldly away. "That Chinese place still deliver? I'm not going out in this cold." he says, as he walks to the kitchen and grabs a beer out of the fridge.

Judith turns to him and her shoulders slump as she sighs. "You're not going to help me tomorrow or the next day. I know you won't." She says softly.

He walks into the room, swigging the beer. "Listen, this decorating is your stuff. Let's just get something to eat. You must be starving, too. I am too tired to argue. I mean, can't you get your 'little group' to help you? You know I have been putting extra time in at the firm." He says, apathetically.

She looks at him coldly with her hands on her waist. "Yes, I am starving but not for food. When was the last time we ever did anything together? You hardly ever look at me anymore. You turn away when we go to bed. On weekends, you go off and don't tell me where you are going. You're always up late on the damn computer doing research 'for the firm.' What about me? Ever since I got out of the hospital, you've been cold and distant!" She says, as her eyes are starting to well up in tears. "My 'Little Group' has been the only ones there for me after I lost the...the baby and..." she puts her hand to her mouth and she starts to sob. She turns away quickly to the lighted tree and John sees her body hitch as she tries to contain her crying.

John sighs loudly and puts the beer bottle on the table near her craft books and walks up to her. He puts his hands on her shoulders gently as he feels her tense up. "Jeez, Judith, C'mon. I'm sorry. Don't you think it was hard on me, too? We have just got to put it behind us." He still feels her tense and she stands frozen in place. "After this Christmas, I will get some time off and we can..."

She squirms away from his touch and turns to face him, her eyes bloodshot, the tears flowing down her face. "No! We won't! It is just another promise that you will not keep. I remember all the empty promises you gave me. I remember how you looked after the miscarriage! It was not grief I saw in your face. I saw relief! All you care about is the fucking firm and how far you can get. Being a partner is all you care about. I have given you so many chances to keep this marriage together. I try and try to convince myself that you will change but..."

"Judith! That is not true. Enough!" He shouts at her, violently. "Do you know how much I work my ass off to pay the mortgage on this place, the bills, credit cards and shit? I have given all I can to you. What more can I give!"

Judith shakes her head, slowly. The rage building up in her. "Oh, I know how you 'give.' Coming home late all the time after 'giving a good fucking' to the office secretary. Don't you dare think I don't know about..."

John rushes up to her and quickly slaps her across the face before she can finish. "SHUT UP!" He shouts as she puts her hand to her reddened cheek with a look of shock. She is silent as he stands in front of her, his fists at his side, shaking, as he says, "You don't know a damn thing! Go do your damn crafts. That is the only thing you care about anymore!" He raises his arms and turns away from her. "When was the last time you supported anything I have done? Huh? You are the one that turns away from me in bed!"

Judith turns away with her face in her hands and falls to her knees before the glowing tree. She is slouched over, shaking, as he looks and walks to stand over her. "There you go. Just turning away again. It takes brass balls to make it in this world. It takes guts you don't have. Don't you see that? You have to be prepared for whatever life throws at you." He says, coldly.

What John doesn't see is how she slowly reaches under the tree skirt. What John isn't prepared for is when Judith rises with a scream, twists around and plunges the butcher's knife into his chest.

*\*\**

It took all the strength she had to pull his body underneath the tree, head first. When he looked down at the handle of the blade sticking out of his chest after she struck, he staggered around the room, trying vainly to get to some sort of way out. He was constantly slipping on the blood that was pooling at his feet. Judith looked on in shock. When he finally fell, the crimson wet floor helped to move him. It was hard to hold his head up with one hand while slashing across his exposed throat with the other so that whatever remaining blood in his body was drained into the bowl of the tree stand. She was grateful that the men who set the tree up gave enough space underneath so she can do this without the fear of tipping the tree over. They followed her instructions perfectly.

After she striped off his clothes and moved his body to the center of the floor in front of the tree, she takes the candles off the mantle and places them at various points around his dead form. She removes all her clothes and gets her craft books from the table. As she kneels in front of his pale body, his skin more pale in the light of the candles and tree, she slowly opens the first book. She is careful not to get blood on the pages and she starts chanting what is written. She holds the knife high above her as her voice gets louder. She closes her eyes and her heart beats with excitement that she tries to contain, knowing what she has to do will take all night. The snow that is gently falling outside the window is like little reflected eyes, watching her as she begins her task.

***

The next evening, Gladys pulls up in front of Judith's house in her Mercedes, the driveway already filled with the equally expensive cars from the other women that arrived before her. They are standing at Judith's doorway near the bay window, the curtains are drawn and a faint glow can be seen of what is lighted inside. The women look at her as she gets out and slams her door shut. Gladys tramps up to the door, her breath a cloud before her as she shouts, "This had better be good. I'm freezing my fanny off!"

The other women laugh and Fiona shouts out, "Your fanny will never freeze off. There is plenty of it!" The women roar even louder as Gladys joins them and says, "Ha-ha, You wish you had this body. Isn't she answering?" Just then, Judith opens the door wide and the women turn to her with pleasant greetings as they enter the warm glow of the foyer. After the exchange of quick hugs and kisses on cheeks, Judith takes their coats and hangs them on the hooks on the wall as the ladies take off their shoes and boots and place them on the mat by the door.

"Well, Darling, what is this fabulous surprise you wanted us to see? I'm sure the girls and I are just dying to find out. You were the most excited we have ever heard you on the phone this morning." Agnes says, with an expectant smile.

Miriam is rubbing her arms to keep warm, also to contain her excitement as she says. "Oh, yes! I have been on pins and needles all day! I cannot even imagine!"

Tabitha looks to her, clutching a large, denim bag to her chest, bulging with a crocheted blanket. "Me either!" She says, with excitement.

Judith folds her hands before her with pride. Her glowing smile is evident as she stands before them. Her body is shining radiantly in a red sequined evening gown as she says with pride, "Well, my friends. I have been working on a very special project just for you. You are my most dear and cherished friends, and I would not have gotten on this enlightening journey if it wasn't for Agnes and all of you. True friends stick by you, thick and thin and words cannot express my thanks to you."

"Please, show us," Tabitha says, "Don't keep us in suspense."

Judith gives a quick wink and says, "Follow me."

They proceed down the hallway to the glow that is greeting them from the living room, Judith leading the way. As they turn into the room, they all stop and freeze. The room is lavishly decorated with an array of holiday colors. Homemade wreathes and tea light holders are placed about in the most artistic of ways and in front of the curtain drawn window is the finished product of the tree.

Hanging on strong hooks all around the tree are various body parts of John. Their pale, bloodless skin is as white as the new fallen snow. Every organ has been meticulously cut and decorated with the most care. A kidney is hanging sprinkled with glitter. Each lung has a silver, lone wide white wing attached to it. Fingers and toes have a small, red ribbon in them as they dangle and turn on the branches. Wrapped all around the tree are his intestines, decorated every few inches with a delicately tied red bow. Different parts of arms and legs encircle the tree skirt with small crevices cut into the muscle and sinew to hold other tea lights. On the top of the tree, in place of a star, is John's eyeless head. His face in a rictus of horror. Two tiny Christmas lights shine out of the sockets as if staring at the women that entered. The eyes, hanging in separate spots in the tree.

The women gasp in shock. Miriam screams. Fiona slowly moves to the loveseat across from the tree and sits down. Her mouth agape. Agnes walks carefully up to the tree and stares at it, her hand to her mouth. Judith looks at all the women, one by one, waiting expectantly for a word of response. Her wide eyes starting to get a look of disappointment. After a moments time, Agnes whispers out. "Judith, what have you done?"

Agnes is still facing the glow of the tree; her silhouette paused in place, as she says again, "Oh my Dear, what have you done?"

All the women turn to Judith and look at her in shock as Agnes turns and looks into Judith's eyes, which are starting to tear in despair. Agnes slowly raises her arms wide and says, "This...is...magnificent!"

The women in the room start clapping loudly. Miriam shrieks again and starts hopping up and down, her hair, waving back and forth. Tabitha goes up to Judith and puts her arm around her shoulder; Judith's tears of despair are now tears of joy. Tabitha rubs her shoulder, comfortingly, and says, "This is so beautiful. I am so proud of you! You have no idea how amazing and gifted you are." Judith closes her eyes in relief as she wipes the tears from her cheeks. She looks to Tabitha with a relaxed smile as Tabitha kisses her on the temple.

Agnes excuses herself and goes to the foyer near her coat as the other women gather around Judith with hugs and encouraging words. Agnes comes back, holding in her hands the small, redwood box.

Judith looks at the box in Agnes' hand, a confused expression on her face. Agnes stands before the tree, facing the woman. "Judith, I am sure all the women here will agree with me that there is no need for a contest. YOU have achieved the ultimate of craftsmanship. You have shown yourself to be a true member of our group."

Just looks at Agnes with a look of pride and humbleness. The women start clapping again and Gladys shouts, "Here, Here!" Judith blushes as Agnes walks up to her slowly.

"My dear," She says, as the women stop their applause, "I have always felt you would become one of us. You just had to take the final leap of faith. No one understands what this season really represents, with their 'made up religions', their fictional Jesus. A savior from an immaculate rape? Hardly!" The women start giggling.

Agnes opens the box carefully. She pulls out a large, black onyx medallion. On it, the evil face of a female demon with a dripping red tongue.

"My great, great grandmother made this in honor of Perchta. She made many for her coven back in the day. This is one of the few remaining in the world. The old ways of our mother are nearly forgotten but there are still a few of us around. We have so much to teach you now that you have found yourself worthy," she says, with a gleam in her eye.

There are hugs all around as Tabitha goes out the room and comes back with the denim bag. She pulls out the contents as Agnes says, "In honor of this night, which I know in my heart of hearts would happen, Tabitha made you a little gift to welcome you to our group." Judith stares in excitement as Tabitha pulls out a large, black crocheted blanket with the symbol of a beautiful, white-haired, demonic woman crocheted in white in the center. Judith gasps in joy as the other woman look at it, oohs and ahh's all around. Gladys is near the tree looking at the work Judith has done and she gazes closely at one of the ornaments and lets out a loud laugh. The women all turn to her as she shouts out, "Ladies, come here!"

They all walk over and they see hanging from one of the branches, two flesh-like orbs wrapped in red and green silk.

Fiona says, "Wait...are those?...Is that?..."

Judith shrugs with a smile, "Well, he always says his were brass, I just thought I would keep them warm."

The woman let out a peal of laughter. They keep laughing as the cold winter's night continues to lightly cover the house and the streets outside with a tender blanket of white. The lights from the tree and the glowing room shine a warmth through the bay window panes that make the accumulating snow sparkle with a magical light that promises to shine all through the night and into the next day.

# The Woman in the Upstairs Window

## By Chris Gonzales

# The Woman in the Upstairs Window
# A True Ghost Story by Chris Gonzales

I was very young when I had two vivid dreams one night. My bedroom was in the upstairs of our five bedroom home, built in the 1900's. The house was huge with an enclosed staircase, we had doors in our walk-in closets that led to other closets and a basement that had been dug out just enough to use as a storage area for canned goods. It was deep with two sets of stairs with a landing where we kept our freezer; it smelled like freshly dug dirt all the time. There was always something about this house that left me with an uneasy feeling. I remember when I'd leave to school, I'd glance back at the upstairs window and always felt like someone was upstairs looking out, watching me. I tried to make it a point never to look up at those windows but sometimes curiosity would get the best of me. When I did look up, I'd see a woman's face in the windows, it was never a clear face but one made of shadows that were cast from the trees or the way the curtains were sometimes left partially opened. It always scared me to look at those windows; she was always there in some form when I did.

The night I had these dreams, I tried to wake myself from the second one more than once, but couldn't. I woke up the next morning exhausted, frightened and confused because the dreams had all felt so real that I wasn't sure if I had actually woken up.

In the first dream, I dreamt a woman had been in a car accident and that she'd been decapitated. I saw her head roll away from the accident and thought she looked a bit like a witch with her pointed nose and chin. As I watched her head roll away from the accident, I realized she looked very much like the woman in the upstairs window I'd seen on our way to school. That frightened me so much I woke up and after some time, I finally chalked it down to believing that I was living in a haunted house. I was determined to leave this house as soon as possible and so, with the newfound understanding and determination of a young child, I fell back asleep.

In the second dream, I am older and still living in the house that I was convinced was haunted. I was joking with someone I didn't know, we were laughing and being silly, I felt safe with this person. In the middle of the laughter and playing, the phone rang and for whatever reason, I stopped playing; the dream went from laughter to frozen fear and somehow I knew this call was to inform us about a death. I wondered how I knew what this call was about; it frightened me knowing that I knew the news before I had been told, even if it was a dream. The person I was with rose and answered the ringing phone. I sat confused in my dream, staring at the person on the phone, watching their mannerism as they spoke on the phone. I could see in their face that the news was bad. They took the phone into their room and closed the door. I tried to wake myself from the dream and thought I could see my sister in her bed across the room, I tried to call out to her but couldn't. I tried to wake up but couldn't, I wanted the dream to end; I was frightened, confused and couldn't wake up; I was in a deep sleep.

The dream continued, the big old house began to close in on me, it felt as though I was watching myself above my own dream. I was sitting in the same spot I'd been playing just moments ago, alone and unable to move, too afraid to move and I thought that odd. I glanced out the living room window and saw that it was dark outside; nobody had turned on the porch light nor drawn the curtains. I was dumbfounded on how quickly darkness had come and began trying to make out the big oak tree in our front yard. The woman's face from the upstairs window began to slowly appear in the leaves of the oak tree; frightened, I turned to look out the dining room window instead. Immediately, I looked down and away from that window too, afraid I'd see the woman's face from the upstairs window peeking in. I stared at the floor afraid she might show up in front of me; the frightened mind of a young child, I sat frozen with fear. I wanted to cry or scream out, anything to wake myself from the dream, I wanted it to end but it wouldn't; the dream continued. The woman's face taunted me as she seemed to appear in the corners of my mind in some ghostly form, she was frightening to look at.

The person who had answered the phone in my dream was visibly upset and when they finally came out of their room; I was sent to mine. I was afraid to go upstairs alone in the dark and I was afraid to look out any of the windows on the way to my room, I was afraid of the woman's image; I kept my head down climbing the stairs. I finally reached my room after what seemed an eternity and looking at the doorknob; I felt grateful for the safety of my own room. I opened the door and the room was a cheerful yellow with light green trims. The curtains are white with eyelets on the ruffles, I stepped inside the cheerful room feeling relieved and thought the nightmare had ended. I looked across the room and out the windows; it was too dark to see anything but darkness. Then, when I looked through the opened closet door, I thought I'd seen the woman's face outlined in the clothes hanging in my closet so I looked away. Curious, I looked again, there she was, the woman I had seen in the upstairs window, clearly outlined in the patterns of my clothes; her head hung as though detached from its body, her eyes were closed, she was obviously dead. The dream became a nightmare and continued.

Ghostly images of the woman's decapitated head continue to float in the darkest corners of my mind. I tried to control the nightmare to make it end and so I decided it was time to confront the woman's face in our windows, I looked again at the closet; she was gone, I felt more in control. I looked at the pretty white curtains with the playful ruffles across the room and walked bravely towards the windows. I put my hands on the curtains and felt the curtain rod, I stood ready to open the curtains and face the evil witch I thought might be outside my bedroom windows. Just as I was ready to open the curtains, I concluded, logically, that I was too young to confront what I believed was a dead witch. In the end, I turned away from my windows, sat on my bed and saw myself fall into my sleeping body. The dreams and the nightmare were over.

I woke up the next morning convinced that house was haunted. I vowed I'd never look up at the upstairs windows again. Of course, over time, I would look up there and each time I did, I saw clear images of the woman's face so I'd look away as quickly as possible. As an older teen, I decided to look at those windows, make sense of the images and chalk it all down to a vivid imagination. I looked at the windows and not only did I see the woman in her usual place but there were other images as well. I looked at all the things outside comparing them to what might cause them to create any sort of the images to appear and while doing so, I saw someone peek out from behind the curtains and the curtains were now opened. I ran into the house to confront whoever was upstairs only to find myself alone in the house, searching for someone that wasn't there.

As time went on, the old house was renovated and we all chose colors for our rooms. I was happy that we were finally ridding ourselves of the drab whites that had made the rooms look dirty and cold. I chose pastels that mimicked spring and because our big oak tree blocked the sun, I painted most of my room yellow.

One night a friend and I were joking around in the living room, we started wrestling over a piece of paper when the phone rang and I immediately felt a sense of déjà vu. I froze while someone else answered the phone. The memory of a car accident I dreamt as a child flashed through my mind. I knew that the woman's face in the upstairs window I hadn't seen since grade school and the woman's head that rolled away from the car accident were the same woman. The call was taken to a private room and the door was closed. The thought that my nightmares seemed to be coming true frightened me. It was late by then and as I glanced out the front window into the darkness, an image of a woman's face began to appear in the outlining of the leaves in the old oak tree. I turned away frightened and realized that my nightmare was unfolding. I tried to change the chain of events in hopes that I was wrong and that the events were just coincidental; that the ghostly image of the woman's face I'd just seen, or thought I'd seen, was a figment of my imagination and nobody had died. I decided to wait to ask what the call was about, something I hadn't done in my dream, or so I thought.

The door to the room opened but before I could ask any questions, I was asked to go to my room. I stood there shocked but seeing there was no room for discussion as the person had returned to their room and closed the door, I went to my room. The longest and most confused night of my life began when I headed to my room upstairs, alone, frightened and confused. Every move I made seemed to be dictated by the dream, every time I tried to change the events; it seemed I was forced by fear to continue living out the dream. I was still frightened by the earlier image of the woman's face I thought I'd seen in the oak tree and felt as though she were following me to my room. I was too afraid to look out any of the windows, so I walked with my head down until I reached my room. When I reached my room and opened the door, I was shocked that the colors matched those in my dream and that the curtains I'd sewn were white ruffled ones with eyelets in the ruffles. I refused to look at the yellow walls with their light green trim and instead, looked into the closet; I saw an outline of a woman's face with her eyes closed, it was too clear to be mistaken and I realized that this event had also been in my dream; I turned my eyes away from the closet and wondered what to do. I was confused and frightened.

Leaving my room was not an option as our rules were strict. I kept trying to convince myself that these events were coincidental and that the news of someone's death was just a dream and my imagination was far too wild. After gathering my courage, I decided to look at the closet again. I saw there was no image of a woman's face. Encouraged, I decided to look out my bedroom windows to further convince myself that there was no image of a woman's face in the oak tree either and I was being paranoid. As I was about to open the curtains, I realized that I was in the exact spot I had been in my dream; frightened too much to open the curtains, I turned and sat on my bed trying to figure out how to make the events of dream stop. I didn't want the news of someone's death to become a reality. As I sat there on my bed, I realized that I was also sitting in the exact same spot I'd been sitting in my dream. I lay on my pillow and started to cry, the feeling of déjà vu was overwhelming, I was still following the exact same events of my dreams and I wanted them to stop. I decided to go to sleep in order to avoid making any more decisions. I hoped that when I woke up, everything would be okay.

I woke up much later to the sound of kids upstairs; they were laughing and asking questions. I went into the room everyone was in and listened to one of the conversations. The girl didn't know why they were there so late at night. They hadn't seen their mother; she didn't come home from work. I knew then that the woman I'd seen in my dreams was their mother and that she had died in a horrible accident. I didn't say anything because I hadn't been told anything, and I was confused wondering why I was so convinced about what had happened. We all eventually went to sleep and woke up to do the morning paper route. The boy that lost his mother and didn't know then helped us with the morning paper route. That morning I was frightened to go on the route but I went anyway. The feeling I was being followed was with me and I felt it was the woman that had I knew had been killed. At some point while tossing papers, I turned to talk to one of the kids on the route and in the bushes, I saw a vivid outline of the woman's face; her eyes were opened and her face looked angry. I was too frightened to finish the route and told the other kids that I was going home. Walking home, I prayed I'd never see the woman again, I never saw her again; I never looked for her again either.

When I was much older, the kid from the paper route and I were talking about his mother's death. I asked him if his mother had been decapitated when her car was struck by the train. He told me she had and asked me how I knew as it had never been mentioned to anyone outside of the immediate family. I told him about the dreams I'd had as a young child and of the night they arrived late in the evening to spend the night with us. I told him how frightening the dreams had been and how strong the feelings of déjà vu were. He told me that I was supposed to tell someone when I had dreams like that. He said it was so that wouldn't come true. I asked him if he was angry with me for not telling anyone and he assured me he wasn't. We were after all, just children at that time. I have had those types of dreams again and I have shared them. Look for more true ghost stories by Chris Gonzales.

Sweet dreams!

Along the Way

By Alan Gravitt

# About the Author

Alan Gravitt grew up in East Point Georgia and graduated from Georgia Tech with a B.S. in Physics and from Georgia State University with a M. Ed in Science Education. Served with the Blackhorse Regiment during the Vietnam War as an Artillery Chief of Section. During his working career, he Taught Physics, Math and Engineering and for 25 years owned or managed several engineering companies focusing on robotics, automation, Water treatment technologies and high strength materials. Other interests include sailing, woodwork and camping.

# Along the Way
## By Alan Gravitt

For over 35 years, his solitary walk in the woods had preceded the joyous Christmas season for Joe Dawson. Sometimes he was gone for a few days, sometimes up to a week. No matter how long his time away, he was always home by December 23rd. He was often asked why he went into the woods alone. He struggled to give a coherent answer without explaining the sense of loss, pain and hopelessness that had preceded his first walk into the woods. Now sixty five years old, Joe Dawson was a remarkably fit man with a head of hair that was mostly grey. He was articulate and open except when it came to his yearly ritual. This had remained his and his alone. In recent years, his son Rob had been especially strong in opposing these solo treks, but had been unsuccessful in ending them.

Joe was unable to say to anyone that the first trip of this long series was to have been his last walk on earth. His life was now so full, that it would have seemed impossible and was impossible now, but then....then was different.

He simply said, when pressed, that he had things to remember and work out. In truth, thirty five years ago, he had intended to walk, fall asleep in the snow, and pass quietly from the life that had been so cruel in the weeks before. He alone had survived the fire that destroyed his home. He alone was dragged out, almost unconscious from smoke inhalation, by a firefighter. He alone lay on the ground gasping for air, restrained by other firemen who watched their comrade rush back into the inferno. That fireman who ran back into the blazing house to rescue his family perished there with them when the second floor collapsed.

Joe knew that he should have been there rather than the fireman. He saw no reason to live. He saw no reason to go loudly either. After weeks of terrible lonely pain, he drove into the high wilderness of north Georgia and then walked, with only a light coat, deep into the cold mid-December woods. He drank heavily from a flask of bourbon, trying to dull the pain and boost his courage and his resolve.

As he had tired from the cold, the exertion and the despair, he found a slight indication of a trail and pressed on relentlessly looking to the summit through the leafless trees and to the firs near the top. They were still green and seemed alive. He hated them. He screamed at everything around him, cursing life, God and the whole damn world for his loss. Finally with his energy ebbing away, he sat against a tree, put his head down and fell unconscious in sleep. A light snow dusted his head. The fall of night was only a few hours away. From time to time, at some almost unfelt stimulus, he roused. A delirium set in with voices and visions both terrible and comforting. He talked to himself and with these monsters and demons and angels until he slipped away, unconscious and unknowing.

When the sun rose the next morning, and the warmth began melting the bits of snow on his hair, he was stunned to be alive. Impossible, he thought. It was almost warm and strangely here he was. As he reconsidered his state, he found there was more. On his lap was a well-worn paper bag and inside this bag was a piece of rough bread and some dried meat, like jerky, and around his shoulders there was a wrap, a threadbare but sufficient quilt. Just enough to cheat him of his plan to embrace the cold. He later learned that a warm front had swept through the mountains that night. That weather change warmed the temperature somewhat above freezing. That with the quilt had been enough.

The sun, streaming through leafless branches, warmed him and its winter brilliance against the snow had been strangely active on his dark spirit as well as his body. He thought of his sister and her family and his envy of them melted away as well. They had been close for years, but he had shut them out since the funeral. Oh, that funeral with the one casket for his wife and the two tiny caskets huddled beside her as they had been in the upstairs hallway, waiting for him, he thought. For over a week, he had not answered the phone or the door at the small hotel where he insisted on staying, alone. His brother in law, Phillip, had actually come to his hotel room, broken in the door, and said gently to him, "Please don't hurt everyone else who loves you. Come back to us."

Joe had sat staring at the wall. He did not answer.

Then his brother-in-law halfway patched the door frame, re-locked the knob lock, closed the door, offered payment to the desk clerk who knew the tragic story, and left in despair.

Now, gazing through a magnificent snow-covered vista instead of a blank hotel wall, Joe had a sudden image of his older sister and her children and of course her husband Phillip.

"Don't hurt the people who love you," he thought.

Still sitting on the ground against the tree, his world revolved.

Life itself stirred in him and he ate the bread. He thought about his chances of making it down. He knew that the energy to go downhill was a fraction of coming up hill. He marveled that he even wanted to go down. He had been so sure. He marveled that there was some hope. He wondered who had come to him as he was sitting against the tree, either late in the day or in the night. Why had they not tried to rouse him? Had they heard him screaming his despair? He had no clue. Then he looked around, half expecting to find someone standing quietly nearby. Nothing, except the small footprints that led up the mountain.

Joe thought that he might go down. Then he thought that he should go down. Suddenly it was clear. He knew that he would go down. No, it was not "would", but that he must go down. The simple act of eating a bit of dry bread had set life back in motion.

For the next 35 years, he enjoyed the gift of a bright and happy future that had once seemed impossible and he never once revealed the dark valley he passed through in the Georgia Mountains. Not all at once, but over the years, he rebuilt it all. After several years, he met his second wife, children followed, and he set the lost family in a vault of his memory and moved on with life.

So now and every year since, just before Christmas, he left it all behind for a few days and walked into the woods to remember who he was, and yes of course, why he was. After that annual time of solitude and reflection, he would drive to a small cemetery near Kennesaw Mountain, just north of Atlanta. There he would spend a few hours with his past sorrow. He would then return to the most extravagant and wondrous celebration of life, family and hope that could be imagined. There, at his home his wife, his son and daughter, two grandchildren, and his sister with all of her family, gathered and shared the season. Never did his wife, Rose, or his two children, both now grown, learn the whole story. They knew of the loss, but not the despair. His sister knew the despair, but even that was unspoken of in the intervening decades.

This December, like every one after the first year, Joe walked into the mountains with joy, not despair. His plan was to be there for several days in the maze of trails that crisscross the national and state forests of north Georgia. This year, a warm sun and a late winter made the time alone beautiful and the mountains friendly and inviting. The details of the woods and trails are not hidden like they are in the snow, he thought. Joe enjoyed the time when snow blanketed the hills, like the first time, but the times like this, with touches of green and life more evident for his walk, seemed more in tune with his love of life today.

His backpack was equipped with all the latest lightweight gear. He had food for a week plus a few days if he was careful. He had to be back in six days to make the beginning of the holiday festivities on time. He knew he would be there.

He camped the first night overlooking a deep ravine and rose with first light to press on the cathartic journey. His camp was a backpacker's camp. A small tent, ground cloth, thin pad to sleep on, a sleeping bag, a small camp stove and a fold out stool to sit on were the only things other than the fire that he had to deal with before moving on. He walked down to the edge of the ravine. Relieving himself on the trail or near the open space that was his campsite would be bad form.

Standing on the edge and looking across the broad slice in the terrain, Joe looked up at the brightening sky. Suddenly a crash behind him caused him to jump around to meet the unknown sound. He realized that a large deer had just broken from the understory of scrub bushes and stopped a few yards from him, snorting with a moist breath that formed a fog in the cool morning air. Joe involuntarily took a step backward. His foot found only a rock with a covering of moss. The rock shifted just enough to upset the aging man's balance. He was in good shape, but age was beginning to take its toll as more and more of his physical agility faded.

His fall down the slope encountered small bushes that slowed but did not stop his descent. A branch ripped his glasses from his face. He didn't notice. Each time he thought he had stopped the slide, a bush snapped under his weight, small branches ripped through his hand and his fall continued. One larger bush seemed to check his fall, but in the process, his grip on it swung him around, smashing the side of his head into a rock. The blackness was instantaneous and complete. He limply rolled the last few yards to the bottom. The whole day passed with moments of consciousness, but without the clarity to understand much more than the pain. He slept or lay quietly, dazed and uncertain of his condition. .

Deep in the night, chilled but not really cold, he roused and became somewhat alert again. Totally disoriented, in pain and very confused, he started to move the only way he knew was toward help, up, out of the ravine. Moving back the way he had come down proved impossible and painful to even try. His blurred and uncorrected vision proved an additional impediment. He stopped, pressed the illumination button on his watch and saw that he had been out almost nineteen hours. *It could not have been that plus a day* he thought. He was hungry, but not that hungry. The few hours to dawn would not be too long to wait. He craved water even more than food, but there was none. He closed his eyes.

Morning light began creeping over the tops of the mountains and the sky changed from shades of orange to a deep blue. A cold front was moving in and was set to stall against some warmer, moisture laden air, pressing up from the Gulf. There would be snow in a few days, and Joe imagined the death that he had chosen so long ago, but avoided.

He started moving. Standing was hard. Sometimes it was easier to crawl than walk

Although he was not thinking clearly he knew that civilization lay downhill. Unable to really sense which way was downhill, he first moved in the wrong direction. Finding an impossibly steep hillside, he started back down and took a turn where he should have gone straight, moving into an adjacent valley that was further from his original path and his car.

He pushed on for another six hours at not more than a crawling pace. He knew that he was totally lost, but he then found a bit of a trail and eagerly followed it. Every dozen yards, he stopped before mustering the strength and clarity to move on.

Hungry and weak, he stumbled into a clearing where a small cabin stood. The cabin had two small windows and a porch with several straight cane bottomed chairs and a few pots with what had been flowers. His head was pounding and his body simply dropped to the ground. Thirty feet from the front porch of the cabin, he closed his eyes.

He was aware that someone was tugging on his coat. Slowly and painfully he was being dragged, a few inches at a time toward the porch. He looked up at a wisp of a woman with silky white hair and a face more like leather than skin. The eyes, however, were as blue as the sky and dancing with life. A smile of great warmth spread across her face as she saw his eyes open.

"You alive, young man?"

He looked up at her and said, "Barely."

He was able to help her by using his hands and feet as she tugged his body up the three stairs to the porch. He tried to sit up, but became so dizzy that he gave up the effort and just scooched along the floor into the cabin. The old woman left him in the middle of the floor, went to a chest and removed several quilts. She arranged them on the floor and maneuvered him onto the makeshift bed. Gently, she placed a folded blanket under his head and covered him with another quilt. She then sat down in a chair a few feet away and breathed heavily for several minutes. Joe closed his eyes and tried to cope with the head splitting pain that restarted inside his skull.

Sometime later, he smelled something that was welcome--food, and when he opened his eyes, she was there with a bowl that had small violet-like flowers on the side, a spoon moved from the bowl toward him.

"Here, sip some of this."

He managed to sit up, and take the first food in two days. It tasted flat and thin, and he promptly threw up the spoonful and dry heaved for several minutes. The woman got a small cloth, cleaned up the spot on the floor that contained the remainder of the food she had given him.

"Let's try this again," she said, refilling the spoon with the thin broth.

And they did three more times before he actually kept it all down. She then fed him a half dozen more spoonful's until he stopped her with a hand raised to stop the shuttling spoon.

"No more right now, please. Maybe more in a little while."

He closed his eyes and noticed that even though there was a small fire in the fireplace, he was cold. He drifted off to sleep. He awoke to find her sitting in a straight chair, dressed in a blue flowered dress with her hands folded in her lap. On a small table beside her was a steaming cup of tea or coffee, her hand on the delicate handle. The cup was the same design as the bowl. Purple violets with ivy entwined circled the cup as she lifted it to her lips, then placed it on the table and moved to his side.

"What happened to you?" She waved her hand, indicating his face that was bruised and scraped.

Joe looked into those blue eyes and said, "I fell." He was wondering how bad his face looked.

"Where are your friends?"

"I was alone."

"Well, that was kinda stupid," she said dismissively, picking up the cup again.

"Do you live here with someone?"

"No, I live here alone. You're not gonna get fresh are you?" she said with an impish giggle in her voice. She laughed quietly and continued, "No, I don't think you could get up, much less get fresh."

Joe looked at this old woman, thinking how that light in her eyes would have easily inspired someone to get fresh decades ago. She was somewhat blurry to him, and he missed his glasses a little more now.

"You're right about that, but most folks know I'm not like that at all. I think you get my thanks today. What's your name?"

"Well, I sure don't know you that well now do I? I got a iron skillet over there if you get any ideas." She stopped and pointed at a heavy skillet hanging from a nail on the rough board wall. Then she laughed. "Looks like somebody done took a skillet to you."

He reached up and touched his forehead wincing in pain at his own touch.

"I'm Annie Farquard, and who are you?"

"Joe, Joe Dawson, Ms. Farquard. You probably saved my life. Thank you for taking me in. "

Annie pulled her straight chair closer to him, arranging her dress just so and smiled, agreeing that she was satisfied with her work saving him.

"You are sorta alone living way up here. How long have you lived here?"

"Almost the whole time since I was born here 84 years ago.

Daddy died here in '82 and Mama died in '96 and I will die here too. "

"Where else have you lived?"

"I lived in Blue Ridge for a few years with my sister. She got the cancer and died, but Mama was not doing well and I came back. I ain't been off the mountain in 11 years. Don't intend to go off again. My grave will be out there with Mama and Daddy. I won't be planted in the city like my sister. No, here with Mama and Daddy. It's gonna be soon now."

"Do you have a phone? I need to check in with my family."

"Got no phone."

"What about a car?"

She laughed, a broad lilting laugh that sounded like a young woman, shaking her head through the amusement. "Do I look like I got a car?"

"How do you get the things you need up here?"

"My sister's boy is a state patrol man. He comes up here every few weeks to check on me. I make a list and he gets it for me. Every few months, he brings a horse or if he can borrow one, one of those four wheel motorcycle things and packs in a bunch of food and candles, matches and paper and the like. He comes up in the summer and cuts a whole mess of wood for the winter. I don't use much but for the cooking and heating, and I pick up small branches that fall when I walk. Don't make the boy cut too much."

"How far is it to the road?"

"I useta could walked it down in about three hours, back up in another five. Can't do that now."

"Well, I don't think I could do that right now either."

Joe smiled at her as she nodded in agreement.

"When I get you a mite stronger and you rest a little, I think you can do it, but my sister's boy won't be back until Christmas Eve. They always come up and spend Christmas Eve a few hours with me. He brings that motorcycle thing with a little trailer and the kids all in it. He borrows it to bring the whole family up. I told you 'bout that, didn't I? They bring a great dinner. "

Annie got up and started across the room

Joe saw a shadow sweep across her face and she began to wobble a little. She quickly lay down on her bed and closed her eyes. He spoke to her several times and she didn't respond except for a little wave of her hand. He tried to sit up but found that he was as unsteady as she was. He sank back onto the pallet of quilts and pulled the top quilt over him, glanced at the fire which was dying down and closed his eyes. They both slept.

Joe woke several times through the night, but went back to sleep. The fireplace was glowing but there was no flame. The embers pulsed with an occasional spark rising and disappearing up the flue. Morning came and Annie brought a cup of tea over and coaxed Joe to try and stand. He succeeded although not easily. They sat at a rough wooden table as light streamed in through the windows. Mornings saw sunlight in the windows, but afternoons the sun quickly disappeared behind the mountain to the rear of the cabin, leaving the one room in deep shadow.

"Why you in the woods by yourself?"

He explained that it was something he did every year before Christmas.

"You got kin?"

He described his wife Lilian, his two children, and his sister and her family.

"Thay a reason you go off by yourself like that. What is it?

He started to tell her that it was none of her business. Thinking that he didn't want to be so rude, he started that explanation that he had told everyone else. She looked at him with those deep blue eyes and he paused. Without really intending to, suddenly it was all spilling out. He recounted the facts of his family in the fire, the fireman, coming to consciousness with everything gone. He laid out the pain, the guilt, the despair that he felt and how each year that passed; he left more and more of the pain in the mountains and rebuilt his life. He did not explain his intention that night thirty five years before.

She looked at him with those eyes, with a compassion that he felt to his core. "Joe, you ain't told the whole story. You ain't told it all. You the boy on the mountain. I know you be him. That ain't important. You got to get to your family. I got to get you saved before I go. I got to get you home to that wife and kids."

She got up and walked out the door and sat on the porch, smiling as she looked out over the valley below.

Joe walked out to the porch and sat down beside her.

"You know I'm dying, Joe."

"That can't be Annie, you seem fine."

"No, Mama died with the heart trouble. Just me and her was here. She told me exactly what it was. How it felt. Where it hurt. I got the trouble just like it. I know my time is over, and now I'm ready to go content.

They talked the rest of the day and into the evening. She showed him the box of papers where she had written her stories. The paper her sister's boy brought her had been stacked up in boxes under her bed. She told him that she had written about her life, her fears and her strengths. She had described the solitude shared with her family. She wrote about the seasons and the hard times they brought. She told him that she had written about what she had hoped to be. She told him about it all, and Joe Dawson crawled into this extraordinary life, and gave her an outside ear that she had not had before. She told him that she believed that the last thing she was intended to do was to be here to get him home. She said that it seemed to her that she had stayed here in her mountains and stayed alive this long for some purpose and didn't know what it was going to be. She cried as she talked about a lost love who died of typhoid when she was twenty. She talked about a life needing to have some value.

Then it was over. She stopped and said, "Eat now and rest now. You're leaving in the morning."

He did. As he walked down the hill, she waved and shouted to him.

"The boy on the mountain is going home." A bend in the trail hide her within minutes.

Although weak and unsteady. Joe worked his way down the trail. He stopped repeatedly and sat for long periods to rest. He was dizzy and his head hurt like the blazes. Five hours later, he emerged on the road and within ten minutes had flagged down a truck and was on his way back to his car. Although his keys were back somewhere on the trail in his backpack, he found the magnetic Hide a Key box hidden under the car and was on his way home.

Arriving home, he walked into the kitchen and Lillian screamed, seeing her husband with a scraped and bruised face and body. After the story was told, she insisted on taking him to the hospital where it was decided that he had suffered a moderate concussion. The attending physician suggested that he be kept for observation and started some anti-inflammatories and antibiotics to deal with the deep abrasions.

By the day before Christmas Eve, he was home and pronounced okay if not well.

He was a strong man and recovered quickly. In a few days he was almost recovered from the near loss of this wonderful life. His thoughts returned to Annie, and a few days after Christmas he decided to go back. He called his son and asked him to take a few days with his old dad for a walk in the woods. They pulled together the equipment necessary and drove north.

As they walked up the trail toward Annie's cabin, Joseph Robert Dawson Jr., Rob to his family and friends, spoke about his worries and extracted a promise from his dad to never go on these treks alone again. He promised to make the time to go with his father in the years to come. At 26, Rob was a strong and perceptive personality, tall and slender, persuasive and logical. He was amazed that after so many years, his dad had agreed to let him come along. Rob did not know that Joe was now, because of his talks with Annie, beyond his need for solo walks in the woods and now focused more on the future than the past.

Rob watched his dad carefully, still looking for some after effects of the damage done just a few days ago. He saw none except the healing scrapes.

As they approached the cabin, Joe realized that there were several people in and around the cabin. A man stood on the porch, several children kicked a ball around the yard and a young woman sat in one of the chairs on the porch. Annie was nowhere in sight.

Joe and Rob walked up to the cabin and the man stepped out a few steps to greet him.

"Hi, I'm Joe Dawson. This is my son Rob."

The very sturdy man with a crew cut stuck out his hand and without much enthusiasm, introduced himself. "Bill Anson, what can I do for you?"

There was an element of "What are you doing here?" in his manner.

"I just wanted to see Miss Annie. She saved my life last week. As a matter of fact she saved more than my life if that's possible. Rob and I brought her a few Christmas things."

Bill looked down, and tears began to trickle down his well-tanned cheeks. The woman in the rocker got up and moved closer.

"Billy, he's the boy on the mountain, isn't he?"

Bill turned to her. "I guess he is, Ruthie. Gotta be him."

He then turned to Joe and Rob and said, "Aunt Annie died this morning."

Joe's heart sank, and his voice was quaking as he said, "She knew her time was coming. She told me that when we talked a few days ago."

Bill put his arm around Ruthie pulling her close and whispered something in her ear. Ruthie disappeared into the cabin."

"We came to see Aunt Annie on Christmas Eve day like always. She was real weak and we stayed, 'cause she wanted us to. Glad we did. Come sit down. I need to tell you how much you meant to her."

Joe was somewhat confused and stammered out, "But it was her, not me."

As they sat down, with Rob sitting on the steps, Ruthie emerged carrying a box and sat down on the edge of the porch. She turned and handed the box to Bill and then looked out across the clearing and swung her legs back and forth like a little girl.

"Aunt Annie was a writer, but she wrote only for herself. She told us all the stories of her life here, but she wrote to remember her own stories. We never saw what she wrote until yesterday when she gave us this box. It was like it was her last will and more so a testament, a story of her life. You run through most of these pages."

Joe was stunned. "That can't be. I just met her a few days ago. She told me stories and that her writing was about her life, but how could I be part of that?"

Ruthie turned around, looked at Joe. "You're the boy on the mountain, didn't you know?"

"I heard her call me that, and you did too, but I don't have any idea what that means."

Bill slightly turned his chair so he was more directly facing Joe. He rocked slowly and then he started. "All our lives, we have known about the boy on the mountain who came into the woods, over 30 years ago, to die. That was you wasn't it?

Joe heard Rob gasp, and turned to see disbelief on his son's face.

"Dad?" was all Rob could say.

Joe sat for a few seconds and then said, "I told her that story last week. I didn't tell her what my intention was, but yes, son, I didn't see a life after I lost my first family. But I didn't know how life could be salvaged just by living on. It was the restart of my life to have lived through that time. I came too close to losing my future and all the joy you, you Mom and sister and the rest of our family have given me. It didn't seem possible."

Rob's understanding rushed in, and he stood to face his father. "That's why you come up here every year. Who knows all that?"

"Until today, no one but myself and I guess Annie. Before last week no one but me. I must have told her while I was delirious."

"There you are wrong, Joe. Aunt Annie shared that time in the snow with you all those years ago, and it's all written down here." Bill said, motioning to the box of paper, "and she spoke of you in stories that she told her family for decades. She didn't know your name. You were just the 'boy on the mountain.'"

Suddenly Joe pictured the small footprints in the snow, thirty five years ago, leading away from where he awoke, and springing from those footprints, the spritely and spirited Annie Farquard.

"I knew someone was there that night, but the chances that our paths would cross again... well, it's almost impossible."

Bill sort of laughed. "But you kept coming up here, year after year."

"That I did. But Bill, I just could not have had an influence on Annie, certainly not a good one."

"Joe, the stories she told us were focused in part on what she did to save you, what you said to her on the mountain that night, and how she imagined your future when she had to leave you. The other part was how she changed by imagining who you were, the pain you had been through and that you survived because of her. She gained some respect for herself and her value that she had lacked before."

"What is to be done with the papers here, Bill? What is to be done with her writing?"

"That is up to you, Joe. She knew you would be back and her wish was that you have the things she has written."

"Don't you want them, Bill, Ruthie?"

Ruthie turned again and answered. "We have the stories she told in our heads, and maybe after you have gone through these papers, I'd like to read them too, but you first."

"Where is she, Bill?"

Bill motioned toward the open door. "Inside on the bed."

"May I?" Joe asked, rising tentatively.

"Sure," Bill said, getting up to lead Joe and Rob inside.

The inside of the cabin was serene with a low dancing fire and Annie Farquard primly lying with her hands folded and just a hint of a smile on her face. As they stood there Bill finally broke the silence.

"We'll be placing her in the ground next to her folks this afternoon. A few other people are coming up. My pastor is coming up to do the service."

Joe looked through the stack and to the first of the neatly numbered pages and sat down to read. The light through the window was enough to read by for a while, and he read quickly and with amazement.

As the morning faded and the afternoon came on, Joe read the account of her encounter with the boy on the mountain. It was matter of fact and strangely detached. She had gone down the mountain to get some medicine for her father who was sick. On the way back she had heard him screaming in despair and had hidden out of his sight. She had watched him stumbling in his drunken state up against the tree. She had come out wearing only a light dress and a quilt wrapped around her shoulders because she lacked a coat. She had some food that she had carried on her long trip down the mountain to the road and into town. She was well known in the area and had caught a ride into town, and her sister drove her back up to the trail. She had squatted next to him for some time, uncertain what to do. The boy on the mountain was so young. He had rattled out the story disjointed and did not respond to anything specific from her lips. She listened to the despair, the self-destructive hatred and the pain. She had covered the two of them with the quilt as she listened. Torn between saving him and getting the medicine she had to her father, she left the quilt and her extra food and headed home. The next day she had returned and found him gone. She had walked to the road and was sure that he had gotten a ride. She had found that his footprints ended at the road and joined with the tread marks of a car in the remaining snow That car must have headed down the mountain, getting him on his way home. She knew he made it home.

Close to a dozen people arrived over the next few hours, most arriving in ATV's, though a small group arrived on horseback, reinforcing the primitive scene. Annie, wrapped in a white cloth, was borne out of her home and gently placed in the grave prepared for her. Each member of the group placed a shovel of dirt in the grave and said a few words of affection. After the service and ceremony, the son of one of her cousins completed the burial, filling the grave. Someone from the town had brought a wreath with colorful flowers that belied the surrounding winter browns. The children promised to plant flowers in the spring, and the assembly began to drift down the mountain. Joe and Bill exchanged contact information and the cabin in the clearing became the sole property of Annie Farquard again.

Joe spent the next week reading the close to 2500 pages of handwritten notes and came to know Annie in more depth and understanding than most would think possible. "Being of use in this life" was a recurring theme.

How could one be of use in such a remote place? Annie was middle age when she found her "boy on the mountain." She had already begun to wonder what her purpose in such an isolated place could be. Her words about her home in the mountains soared and inspired, though none had read them before. Then the hope of her words faded.

The spring is so gracious in its beauty. I love watching every bud around here opening and showing me what's inside. The green and the spots of color cheer me up. Even though the leaves mean I can't see as far, the things to see up close are so grand, that it seems the mountains and all are here just for me and mine. It is lonely here all the time but for the hills and what's on them. Should I go down and die there, or stay here?

Joe wondered how she had been taught to write with what was mostly correct English. He wondered if the few books in the cabin included a primer on grammar. He had noticed that there was a worn dictionary. Maybe that was it.

She wrote.

"It's hard living in this place. Just livin is hard, keeping warm is hard, eating is hard and caring of kin is hard. Thinking why I were put down in this place and this time is hard. I think that I was put here to be of value for something, but I shall not marry ner pass on to my children what goes on in my head and heart."

This was dated the year before she found him dying in the woods.

The papers were mostly in order. She only recorded the year with no month or day. Each page was numbered up to two thousand five hundred and seventeen. That seemed strange at first, but then he realized that maybe she didn't know dates, just seasons. He wondered if she had kept a calendar and just didn't record the date. *"What did it matter?"* he thought.

The transition to the new year in the dark of winter was obviously difficult. At one point she observed.

"The snow has been on us for three weeks. Daddy is sick again and I have to bring in the wood. I can't get away from the insides of this cabin. I think I'll die afore this winter is gone."

But winter did pass and with it a rise in her spirits. The garden occupied her time and she wrote about each thing that happened in great detail, the harvest and putting things by. Canning with her aging mother and father was recorded as the seasons marched by. An occasional trip down to town punctuated an otherwise uneventful autumn.

Winter brought back the despair that she felt as the busy and green time faded.

I'm just living and eating and breathing and writing, but I'm not sure I'm really going to keep living. I don't have a value beyond this place. The whole world is out there and I'm afraid I can't ever connect to it to show it that Annie has some value to it. Problem is I just don't like it down there. It scares me, so I'll die here without a mark on that other place.

Then the day that she returned from her trip down off the mountain and found him.

He was screaming, cursing and moaning. He was hurting so much. I knew from what he was raving about that he was trying to leave this life to end the pain. He had been drinking too. I didn't dare come up to him, so I watched until he calmed down against the tree, He looked dead and I came out and walked to him. He was just a boy it seemed. I sat beside him and spoke but he didn't hear me, not really it seemed, but then he started talking about his lost love and little children, burned in the fire. I cried to hear such a story. I thought that maybe I would die there with him. Somebody should not die so alone, but then I had to go and get Daddy his medicine. I had to leave the boy on the mountain and save Daddy. I just had to, so I warmed him with the quilt and left some food I had not ate on my trip. I promised him I would be back in the morn. I don't think he heard me. I did go back and he was gone, not dead, gone walking down the path. I walked after him. I thought he might drop and I could be there to save him. I went all the way to the road and, glory, he was gone in a car that seemed like had stopped to pick him up. The footsteps was there and the tire tracks was there and he was gone. Maybe what I did saved him. No, I know what I did was of value to the boy I found on the mountain.

From that point on her writing was never again dark and morose. Even the winters were filled with joy. She wrote about his life. Projecting her hopes on his unseen life. She wrote about his romance with an imagined lover. He blushed as he read about re-found love and passion. The story was not really accurate in its detail, but was the age old story of life and love. She wrote about his work and how he helped people. Again not accurate in detail, but with elements of a good life well lived. She offered a chronology of love, marriage, children and work. She wrote of his life, missing the dates, missing the number of children and missing so many things in her imagination, but capturing the life she had saved. Her value was assured in this life as was his.

Over the decades, through the seasons and the life and death of her own family, she imagined his happiness of his life, and reveled in her certainty of her contribution to that life. Her life, the joy and the sorrow, was chronicled alongside his as she imagined it. She revisited her dark times as she experienced the same symptoms of heart failure she had seen in her Mama. She wrote of her death, not in a fearful or grim way, but as a finish line event to a life that she took pride in. A life elevated by saving the boy, and knowing, imagining, hoping that he did well.

He reached the last few pages. These were folded and wrapped in tissue with a blue ribbon and a note, with the words, "For the boy, now the man, Joe Dawson. Read this last please. "

Joe knew that what was contained here was written after he left, in the days before she passed on. He had read all that she had written and knew that these last few pages were just for him. He set them aside for a few days before spending that last time with Annie.

When the time came, he asked his wife to plan a dinner and invited his son Rob and daughter Alisha to come for the weekend. Alisha came from Macon and stayed at the house with them. Rob came in from Conyers for the day. They all knew that Joe had been reading for weeks and that now, he was ready to share with them what all this was about, but Rob alone had an understanding of just how this was developing.

After dinner, Joe looked around the table at his life's work arrayed. He put his hand on his wife's hand

"My dearest, you know I love you beyond words. You are the light of my life and my companion of a lifetime. Rob, Alisha, I am so proud of you and I cannot imagine a better son and daughter."

He then put his head down and wept, thinking of his lost first love and the lost children that seemed so close at that moment, yet gone forever. No one spoke, but they surrounded him knowing with certainty what caused the tears.

When his composure had returned, he moved to his purpose. "We are all here today because of something that happened thirty five years ago. A chance meeting in the mountains with someone you have never met made this life possible."

He tapped the ribbon-tied papers in front of him on the table. "I don't know what is in here, but we will all find out today the words to us from the woman who saved my life twice."

Joe reached for the ribbon, untying the simple bow and unfolding the few pages. He sat looking at the pages. He saw a frail and uncertain handwriting that filled two and a half pages and considered the effort required to make this last demand of a failing body. He began to read.

Joe. I know you will come back, but I don't think I will still be here. The chest pain is real bad and it's just a sign to me that I won't be here. Billy will get this to you. He promised me that.

When I found you this time, it was like when I found you before, except this time you was wanting to live. Last time I was wanting you to live, but you wasn't wanting to live, but you did anyway. I believe that the only reason that you wanted to live now is that I wanted you to live the last time. That was part of my value in this life. I hope you don't mind that I made up your story. I didn't ever expect to see you again, but when you came back I knew who you were right away. That first night I had looked at your face and the same face was what you have now, but the pain was not there like it was before. I almost told you the whole story, but didn't want to seem to be bragging that I was the one who found you before, but I want to tell you that I took saving you to be the best thing I had done in life and made up how good I done and how good your life was, and your children and your wife and your work helping folk. I got it wrong, 'cause it was better than what I wrote 'cause what I wrote wasn't true. What I wrote was just me getting through life with some prideful thought of what I done that made a difference outside these mountains. I am sorry if I did that wrong. Instead you wrote your own life, your own wife and children and your own work. You traveled and saw things. You were good to people and I saw it when you told me about your family. You can hide an evil spirit, but a good heart shows.

With that Joe stopped and handed the papers to Rob. "I can't Rob, would you finish?"

Rob took the last sheet, struggling to read the script there, and in a soft voice read.

I guess I should tell you that you saved me too. I was not being joyful in the hard times but after I knew that you got down the mountain safe, I knew that I would get through to my end safe too. And I did. Then you came back and just when I was getting into that dark death time, you told me your real story. It was like you came when I needed you and your real story the most, and I could go on to the grave knowing that I did some good and that you did some good with what I gave you. That's all we can do in this life, try to do good by those we meet on the mountain and help them along the path. Thank you for doing the same for me.

Rob finished and handed the pages to his Dad, and Joe set them beside his plate and tapped them gently.

"It's hard to consider how much we owe people who we never knew and might never have known but for chance. Annie made this family possible, that is for certain.

Joe and his family ate quietly, loved each other and then went on with their lives. They tried just a little harder to be of value, knowing the fragility of life.

Four years later, Joe Dawson died trying to pull a family from a car sinking in a cold winter's lake. He got two children out and went back for the mother and baby. He didn't make it out and died alongside a woman and child he did not know. As Rob was going through his papers, he found a journal that Joe had started after reading Annie's pages. These along with many of Annie's notes and with Rob's own notes about his father's life and death were published a few years later by the man whose two children were saved. He was an editor for a large publishing house and thought the stories that led from tragedy in a house fire forty years before to a cabin in the wilderness and then to his own horrible loss, were of value. It was titled

"Being of Value: Life and Joy Along the Way."

After holding that book in his hands for the first time, Robert Dawson sat at the keyboard and began to type in earnest, telling stories. The stories were only about the good people in life, both real and imagined. Rob typed fearlessly, hoping to be of value.

Christmas Massacre
By Sheri Ann Richerson

Sheri Ann Richerson is a leading pioneer in the self-sufficiency movement. For the past 19 years she has been living, teaching, and promoting organic gardening, natural health and self-sufficiency through all forms of media. Her career includes years as a nationally acclaimed best-selling author, radio host and guest on a variety of shows – showcasing her expertise on homesteading and gardening. Additionally, Ms. Richerson is a speaker, columnist and a blogger for hundreds of websites, magazines and newspapers. Sheri lives in Marion, Indiana. For more information, please visit her writing website at SheriAnnRicherson.com, her gardening website at http://www.exoticgardening.com or her homesteading blog at experimentalhomesteader.com. Be sure to subscribe to the Experimental Homesteader podcasts on iTunes.

Sheri Ann Richerson

Author - #1 Best Seller Complete Idiot's Guide to Year-Round Gardening,

Complete Idiot's Guide to Seed Saving & Starting, 101 Self-Sufficiency Gardening Tips & more! http://www.experimentalhomesteader.com

# Christmas Massacre
# By Sheri Ann Richerson

What began as the happiest night of the year quickly turned into a bloody massacre for the people who lived in the city of Lost Angels - that's how the newspaper article began. We all know now that's what people were meant to believe. It was believed that everyone who was in the town that night was murdered either by poisoning, beheading or gunfire. The only known survivor had been behind bars for years now. The newspapers, radio reports and even the TV news anchors had eerily dubbed him the Grim Reaper right from the beginning. No one knew his name – not at first - but everyone was sure he was the only person who had escaped that night.

Unknown to everyone, including the Grim Reaper himself, there was one other survivor. She was a 12 year-old girl who had been seen as an outcast by the townspeople. She had seen it coming and was able to escape undetected surrounded by the cloak of darkness. She was the only one at the Christmas celebration dressed in black, hidden in a far corner of the room. The other children ignored her and the Grim Reaper, dressed as Santa Claus did not see her.

Santa Claus arrived that night in a timely fashion – as he had every year prior. This year something seemed off to Natalie. As the festivities began, she noticed Santa Claus was passing out treats to all the children. That was something new and it struck her as odd. The tables were filled with cakes, cookies and all kinds of Christmas candy. What was this Santa Claus up to, she silently thought.

As the children began eating the treats, she noticed something was changing. Silence was filling the air. The children were falling asleep. Something was wrong. This Santa Claus had handed out some kind of deadly treat to all the children, all except her. Even the adults at the party were falling asleep. The only one still alert, besides herself was Santa Claus. She knew she had to go for help – but she had to avoid alerting him.

As the children and adults continued to slump into piles on the floor, one-by-one, Santa Claus turned his back to her. This was her chance. She crept silently along the shadows near the wall, staying as close to the floor as possible, stopping every couple of feet to look at him. She had to know she was not detected. Thank goodness she always wore black. That made it so much easier to hide in the shadows.

As she neared the rear door of the building the lights went out. She heard a commotion near the front doors and realized some parents had come for their children. Now she could make a break without being detected. She slowly eased the back door open just wide enough for her tiny body to slip through. She then carefully closed it to make sure it did not bang. She wanted to avoid detection at all costs.

While she was had been sneaking through the rear door, the Grim Reaper had removed the Santa suit and replaced it with black clothing. He had a plan. He watched from the shadows as the parents filled the dark room. He smiled as they screamed and cried wondering why their children would not respond. It was at that moment that he realized there was a rear door – and he knew that could ruin his plan.

With all the confusion and the darkness, it was easy for him to move about. His first step was to lock the front door and then slowly navigate through the crowd to lock the back door. With no electricity there was no way the people of the town could call for help. Even though everyone had cell phones, they didn't get good reception in the city of Lost Angels. The Grim Reaper was aware of this and he knew this was his moment to strike and strike he did.

First he wanted to take out the ones who could defend themselves. Most of those people were now locked in this building. He had hidden several high-powered military guns in this building, so all he had to do was locate them and open fire. The shots rang out into the silence of the night. No one stood a chance. He laughed the most evil laugh imaginable as they were blown apart. He loved watching their blood and body parts litter the room. Once no one was left alive, he put the gun down and walked out into the street as though nothing had happened. He had more one stop to make before the night was over.

His next stop was the old folks' home. He had a special treat for them. He laughed as he slit their throats, one by one. He watched the elderly and the sick collapse in a pool of their own blood. He loved watching the faces of the ones still alive. The look of horror and fear on their faces excited him. There was no one left alive who could stop him.

As the midnight bells started to ring, he let out the most evil laugh Natalie had ever heard. She was hiding in the darkness at the edge of town. She began to shiver uncontrollably. That laugh was the most fearful, most evil sound that she had ever heard. At this point, she was no longer sure if this person who had pretended to be Santa Claus was from this world or from some other world.

She was glad she was not part of the crowd that night. She had not been feeling well and had asked to stay home, but it was tradition that any child under the age of 16 went to the children's Christmas event. She had just turned 12 a month prior. Since she was forced to attend, she had decided to just sit in a dark corner, alone that night. No one noticed – no one cared. She had not wanted to deal with the bullying – and now it seemed she was the only one alive. Even her younger brother and her younger sister didn't make it out alive.

When she had first escaped the party she had planned to head home to tell her parents that something wasn't right but she never made it. She knew as she heard the gun shots ring out into the night, that this was a night like none other. This was when she decided to run for the cover of the woods. At first, she intended to run until she made it to the next town, but she didn't know who she would tell there or what might become of her when they found out she was an orphan. One thing she was sure of was that if she turned back now, if she went back into the town, she would be dead.

She found a hollowed tree trunk to hide in, and waited silently though the night. As daybreak came she didn't know what to do. She knew she should have walked into another town, but fear held her back. Finally she realized she had to move on. She walked until she reached the next town. That was when she found a little convenient store to go into. The newspapers were already buzzing with the news of last night's events. She picked one up and sat down to read it.

She knew she couldn't go home. The authorities were on the hunt for the Grim Reaper, as they called him. In order to stay alive, she had to avoid him. She did not know who he was and feared he might recognize her. In order to survive she somehow had to make it on her own. Who would believe her? Where could she go? She quietly pondered these thoughts.

She put the paper down, glanced up at the TV that was playing behind the counter in the convenience store and saw video footage of the people she knew laying in pools of blood. She shivered again and headed off into the woods towards a tree house that have been a favorite playing spot of hers. She knew these woods well. She knew the berries and other wild plants she could eat. She knew how to collect and roast the nuts. She knew how to fish, de-bone and cook the fish over an open fire. Her parents had done quite well teaching her survival skills, even though she had assumed she would never need them. Suddenly those skills including the skills she had worked on during hunting season, seemed necessary for her survival.

She had no money and no one she could be sure would help her in town. She knew for sure she wasn't going back into Lost Angels to look for anything. After all, the Grim Reaper could be hiding there, waiting. She headed towards the tree house, gathering wood, berries and nuts as she went. It would be a while before she ventured back into the new town. She didn't want to take the chance of being caught by an adult or authority figure or worse, the Grim Reaper as he was now known.

From time to time, just to see what the newspapers had to say, she wandered into town. No one seemed to notice her or ask her any questions. She waited patiently - patiently for news that the Grim Reaper had been caught. The days turned into years. The seasons kept changing. It seemed that terrible Christmas Eve was no longer on anyone's mind – except hers.

As the years went by, she lost track of time. The only way she knew what day or month or year she was living in was when she went to town to see the newspapers. She bathed in the stream. She had learned how to make soap years ago from wood ashes and animal fat. She avoided people. No one seemed to care that the tree house was there so she had a safe haven. No one even seemed to realize that the tree house was occupied. Then again, she tried hard to keep a low profile. As much as she wanted to go back to the city of Lost Angels – just to see what was left or if it had been rebuilt, she knew better. Deep in her soul she trembled every time the idea popped into her head.

Then one day when she went into town, there was the headline that she had been waiting for. It had been over 3 years since the massacre happened. She was 15 now – but at long last, the Grim Reaper had been caught. She was free from the terrible thought that he would find her. The opening paragraph said he laughed about killing all those innocent people. The headline said it was his plan to destroy every person who lived in the city of Lost Angels and destroy them he did on a night when they were happy. On a night when they were worshipping their God – who he quickly said did not protect them. On a night when they were surrounded by family - and yet no one was safe, not a single soul – except Natalie because she had been an outcast of society.

The Grim Reaper was quite sure no one had survived. He had no idea she had successfully escaped and had survived more than three years on her own living in the woods. In just three more years she would be of legal age and could go back into society without any questions being asked. At first - now that he had been caught -she wanted to go back to the city of Lost Angels. Back to her parents' home. There were some things that she needed – and some things that she wanted. She wondered what life there was like now.

Natalie decided it would be best to go back in the dead of the night. She didn't want to take a chance of getting caught. She didn't know if anyone was living in the city now or if it still abandoned.  Cautiously, she silently made her through the darkness down the main street of the city towards her old home. It seemed the town was still just as it had been on that fateful Christmas Eve. She had feared that new people had come and settled in the city. That the items she desperately longed for were forever lost.

As she walked along, trying hard to stay in the shadows – just in case others were there - flashbacks of that night returned. The joyful Christmas music that the carolers were singing seemed to flow all around her. She could hear the children laughing and playing.  Then she heard the gunshots ring out again, the evil laugh and the Christmas bells towing at midnight. Her fear reared its ugly head and the smell of blood filled her nostrils. She quickened her step but her fear won. She had to stop – just for a moment. She had to gather herself. She knew she had come this far and she had to continue on. She had to go back to her home. She had to see if anything was left.

As the anxiety subsided, she began her journey once again. She found herself outside of her parents' home. She looked in the windows, but the home was just like it had been left. She quickly opened the front door and slid inside. She then ran to her room. She found her birth certificate first. She knew she would need that. Then she looked in her secret hiding spot and found some money she had been saving up. She took it as well and just quickly as she came, she left. There was no point in lingering – but on the way out, she grabbed the last family photo that had been taken. It was the only reminder she would take.

She had been lucky over the past three years that she had been able to find clothes by going through peoples' trash late at night in the other city or by looking through the dumpsters. She had been able to take those items without being caught. She had just three more years to go - three more years until she could legally be free without questions being asked – and she knew now that she would make it to her 18th birthday.

As the years passed, she found herself a job, saved up some money and moved to a large city where no one asked questions about her past. The years came and went. She remained alone. It was easier that way. She did not celebrate Christmas – but did light a candle every year on Christmas Eve, right before midnight, in remembrance of that fateful night.

Life was lonely – but good – until the news came that the man known as the Grim Reaper would be set free. It had been 40 years now since that fateful night, and sometimes it seemed like it had been an eternity since it had happened. Sometimes it seemed like a bad dream - a bad dream that wouldn't go away. Even so, she could still hear the laugh, feel the fear, smell the blood – these memories just would not go away. There was only one thing left to do – and so she made the phone call, setting her carefully laid plan in motion.

The day finally came – the day when she would face the Grim Reaper. She had found the strength to come forward, to tell the truth, to prove who she was and to let the world know that she had survived the massacre on that Christmas Eve so many years ago in the city of Lost Angels.

As she stood – waiting for him to arrive – she prayed, asking for strength to endure what was about to take place – asking that she had the courage to go through with the plan that she set in motion – but most of all, asking that no one who was innocent would be harmed.

As the Grim Reaper approached, she realized he was no longer a towering hunk of a man. The years have not been kind to him. He was frail and he looked as though a big gust of wind could push him over. He looked sad. The years had indeed taken a toll on him and maybe the evil deeds he did that night finally caught up to him. That was what she thought has she faced him down, as she told the story from the eyes of a 12-year-old who ran and remain closed in darkness out of fear for her own life. Yes, she was a child that night that turned into an adult by morning. She had managed to spend the next six years on her own and survive. He had forced her to grow into an adult fearful of all those around her.

She could never forget what she witnessed that night. She would never forget what had been taken from her and today - at this moment - was her chance for justice, her chance for revenge. It was Christmas Eve - the day she chose - the day that seemed right to her. She had grieved and suffered; now it was his turn. Now he was going to pay.

No one knew her plan but she had thought about it carefully and now she waited - just as he had waited that night - just as he had passed out the poison candy - just to see each child eat their treat. He knew that they would pass quickly into darkness and death. He watched, delighted as each adult was slaughtered. Now it was his turn to meet his maker and answer for his evil deeds.

She knew she didn't have much time left to live. The years had taken a toll on her too. Her last act in this world, on this Christmas Eve, all these years later was going to be making him pay. She had managed to gain access earlier that day into the room they would be meeting in. She had tainted the pitcher the water would be served in. She knew drinking the poison would cause him to die a slow terrible death. She knew that she would come under suspicion, especially if anyone else tried to drink out of that pitcher - but it was okay, her days were already numbered.

His dark, beady eyes looked her over once he sat down in the room. No - he didn't recognize her - how could he she wasn't a child any longer? She reached out to pour water from the picture and then she smiled at him. She knew this would be the last thing he would ever drink but then she stopped. He looked her over again and the corners of his mouth turned up.

"You escaped, didn't you? You survived the Grim Reaper - yet here we are together again on Christmas Eve," he said with an evil drawl.

Natalie thought the surprise is on you - but she was wrong - his companion was every bit as evil as him. He had a machete hidden inside his trench coat. He pulled it out quickly and Natalie's head was severed. They were alone in a private room. That was her first mistake. Never underestimate the devil himself. It all happened so fast there was no where she could run this time. But she got the last laugh because the lawyer and the man known as the Grim Reaper drank the water together to celebrate killing the last survivor of the city of Lost Angels.

The Kindom Art Murder

By Ian Bush

Ian Bush pictured with his wife, Samantha.

Ian Bush has been writing stories for twelve years. His first self-published novella *This Story Has Soul* was released in 2010. His novella *Wishes For The World Around You* was published from a 2012 writing contest ran by 2 Moon Press of Marshall, Michigan. In 2013, Ian was a contributor to the anthology *Satan's Holiday*. In 2014, you can see Ian published in the first and second issue of *Shadows and Light Anthology* and *Blessings From the Darkness*, an anthology published by Black Bed Sheet Books to help support best-selling author Yvonne Mason fund for her son's undiagnosed illness. You can also find him in *Spectral Hauntings II, BRAINSSSSS III,* and *Don't Look Back*, an Urban Legend anthology, published by Dark Moon Press this year. Ian Bush is currently spending his days writing in various projects and enjoying his time with his wife, Samantha. To contact Ian Bush, find him on Amazon, Facebook as Author Ian Bush, or send him a personal email at Iancbush@Gmail.com.

# The Kingdom Art Murder
## By Ian Bush

Her name was Klaudis. That is all Gary needed to know. Klaudis was a petite strawberry blonde, and Gary wanted her in his life. Klaudis was seventeen, Gary was twenty one. She was a model who was going to do things in life; he was a man with a greasy mullet. Even if Gary wished for her this Christmas with his entire being he still wouldn't have her as a girlfriend. Klaudis and Gary met and worked together at the Kingdom, a theater for the various arts. She was a concession stand attendant, charming people with her picture perfect smile. Gary just kind of floated, symbolic to his life. He never knew which crowd he belonged to, just kept changing like a chameleon into the group he was with at that point in his life. Gary would stare from his various tasks around the theater, just waiting for her to flash that smile his way. She always did, Klaudis felt a certain pity for poor Gary. She knew she was hot shit, could get any man in high school she wanted or desired. Yet, she would smile that perfect smile that mommy and daddy paid thousands to create and wonder why she was so attracted to this weird man.

Matthew Polson, or Mayor Polson as many called him, smiled from ear to ear. Christmas time was his favorite time of year, the time where he could use his fortune to give back to his loyal constituents. He sat in his office and kept himself frozen in this joyful moment. His bodyguard, a 6'5" bear of a man, stood at the front door of the office.

"Boris," Matt kept smiling, regarding his loyal, stone faced body guard. He grunted in response.

"You have served me well." Matt stood up, walking to the window and cracking it open. Matt opened a small cigar chest that was by the window, grabbing a cigar the size of his thumb. He clipped the end of the cigar, pulling out his metal Zippo lighter from his pocket. After lighting and inhaling deeply, he exhaled and looked at Boris again.

"Boris, Boris, Boris." He muttered. Boris stared at him intently.

"Boris, it is three days before Christmas. Let's go to the spa." Matt chuckled at Boris as he raised a questioning eyebrow.

"Relax, my friend. Let's go relax in the sauna. I will hear no rebuttal from you. I don't expect you will give much of one anyways." Matt stubbed his cigar out on the ash tray, closing the window and leaving the tray there. He then went to the coat rack, grabbing his fur lined jacket and putting it on, pushing the hood up onto his head.

"Boris, I will hear no more of your resistance!" Matt spun the bodyguard to the door, "Snag the car. We have places to be." Boris huffed, opening the door to the secretary's area.

"Leaving so soon Mayor Polson?" The secretary smiled. She was a young knock out, a slim black skirt complementing her curvy frame.

"Go home Meghan."

"Sir?" She questioned. Boris went outside, embracing the cold as he walked down the street.

"Damn you all and your puzzled looks. It is three days before Christmas! Go home!" Mayor Polson walked around the secretary's counter and grabbed Meghan's overcoat. He pulled it off her chair and wrapped it around her shoulders.

"Mayor?" She asked again, rising to her feet.

"Go go go! Don't come back until after New Year's. That is punishment for questioning me." Matt patted her on the shoulders, a grin from ear to ear.

"Yes sir," she tied the belt around her overcoat, grabbing her purse and walking around the counter to shut the lights off. Meghan looked slyly behind her before she left.

"I will see you on Christmas, at the Empire?" Matt looked up quickly, too engrossed with the figure of his sectary and not expecting the question.

"Of course. See you then." Matt smiled, raising his hand. Boris arrived at the front door, holding it open for Meghan. She smiled and left, lost in the blinding white snow within seconds of her crossing the street.

"Sir, your car is ready. The storm is bad though, I don't suggest this."

"Boris," Matt patted him on the arm, "it is two blocks down the road. We will drive safe. Come now." Matt locked the door.

"After you." He smiled, again assisting Boris out of the door.

Mica stared out the window of the second floor of the Kingdom. She watched as the Kingdom flashed its lights with dancing bulbs, watched as the cars drove by, slowly making its way through the blizzard. She let out a sharp sigh, going to her office on the corner of the building. She grabbed the remote off her cluttered desk, turning on the television. She turned it onto the news.

"The weather forecast will be partly cloudy tonight, with a temp of -20. Tomorrow will be sunny, with a high of -10. Christmas eve will be slightly blustery as well, but will hopefully clear up overnight for a Christmas sunny day. The current temperature is -35 with heavy snow showers."

"Fucking better clear." Mica clicked off the television, looking back outside. She could barely see her car parked on the opposite side of the street, but could see the pile of snow forming on the street. She huffed once more, going to her closet. She pulled out her blankets and pillows, throwing them on the couch in her office. She went back to the closet, where an oak wine cabinet was. She opened the cabinet, pulling out a wine bottle and a glass.

"God forsaken snow and the drinking problems that come from it." She put a corkscrew into the top of the bottle, twisting it until she could put the lever down and easily uncork the bottle. The deepness of the red wine escaped from the bottle, filling her lungs with inebriating warmth.

"Mica!" An echo went around the theater. She hissed loudly again, continuing to pour the wine at an angle into the tulip glass.

"Mica!" The echo called out again, the voice's accent made Mica's name sound like "Meeka." Mica hid the bottle back in the oak cabinet, closing the closet door and walking out of her office. She went through the common space to go into the open sound booth overlooking the theater. She scanned the 960 seats, looking towards the stage. A woman walked around on the main stage, barely seen from the dim lights. Mica grabbed a house spotlight and shined it at the woman.

"Syn," Mica chuckled, "what are you doing?"

"Vell," Syn was looking into the spotlight, "I knew you'd be here." Her thick Russian accent echoed throughout the theater. Her icy blue eyes shined in the spotlight, she wore a furry, puffy jacket. Her black hair was short, which flipped away from her face when she turned her head. She had slim features and very long, slender legs that made her beauty even more unique.

"God you Russian starlet." Mica shut the light off, going back into the main common space. She pulled a chair from the square table in the middle of the room, spinning it to the windows and kicking her feet up on the window sill. Mica tried to pose, seemed like the story of her life, to always look as if she was posing for a dramatic photo. Syn's long heeled boots clicked off the steps, then off the wood floor behind Mica.

"Vuata doing here?" Syn asked as Mica turned a curious eye behind her back.

"I could ask the same."

"You live here or something?" Syn chuckled at her joke. "Is that vwine?"

"Yes, it's wine." Mica annunciated the word.

"Vou are exotic too, you know?" Syn walked over and snatched the glass out of Mica's hand. Mica chuckled, reflecting on how her heritage was quite unique. Her father was true Persian, her mother a Native American tourist who fell in love with the sharp features of her father. Mica had long, black hair with jagged facial features. She looked in the window's reflection as she noticed her tiny body, honed by muscle just visible outside the red V-neck sweater she wore.

"What are you doing here?" Mica asked again.

"Vell I live a block away, I vanted to send out our e-mail about Christmas."

"Couldn't use your internet and lap top from home and do that so you could miss this storm?"

"Meeka, Meeka. I missed my favorite theater director, who I knew would more than likely be here."

"I see." Mica went to her closet in her office again, grabbing another wine glass and pouring herself another.

"Vat is this?" Syn pointed at the pillow and blankets on the couch.

"A couch. With blankets. And a pillow." Mica looked at Syn, who was trying to decipher the true meaning.

"It's bad out, I'm not risking going home." Mica retreated to the comfort of her desk, distracting herself by organizing papers. She noticed the envelope with "EVICTION" in red letters, which she quickly hid below the stack.

"Meeka!" Syn gasped, Mica's head snapped up with wide eyes.

"What?" Mica asked in fear.

"This place is a mess, so unlike you."

"Did you seriously walk a block from your house to critique my office?" Mica snapped.

"No Mika, it's three days before your Christmas."

"My Christmas?"

"Christmas is different in Russia."

"Oh?"

"It is celebrated on January seventh."

"Interesting fun fact of the day." Mica chuckled. Syn sighed heavily.

"I'm lonely." Syn plopped on the chair adjunct from Mica's desk. Mica sighed, sitting in her leather chair.

"Me too." She mumbled, sipping at the wine.

"There should be a place vere all the lonely people meet."

"There is, it is here."

"I see no one but us."

"But," Mica swooped an arm over the theater, "this is a safe haven for all types of people. I sacrificed so much to keep this place alive for the lonely people to go where they are surrounded by art and by companionship."

"You have done vell." Syn pointed at all the hanging frames of newspapers and framed reviews of the Kingdom.

"Sometimes I don't feel like that." Mica felt a pang of guilt, knowing still what was under that pile of papers on her desk.

"Meeka, you are a young and successful business owner. You have beauty and charm. I'm vnot surprised why the Mayor picks the Kingdom for your Christmas. It's vonderful."

"It can be at times."

"To the place for all the lonely people." Syn tilted her tulip glass.

"To the lonely place." Mica smiled and toasted.

Matt sat in a steaming hot tub with a smile across his lips, the mist and steam floating inches above his head. He sank deeper into the hot, numbing water. Boris sat; arms crossed and back straight, in the hot tub.

"Jesus Boris, get the fucking board out of your back and relax a little." Matt laughed. Boris growled, sinking in the water a little more, but still straight as a board.

"A little better I suppose." Matt smiled, looking at his awkward and uncomfortable friend. A Japanese woman came by, wearing a traditional oriental blue dress.

"Hello Mayor," she smiled, her features soft and young.

"Why hello."

"A drink for you?" She asked.

"What do you recommend on a cold day like this?"

"We have great tea sir."

"How about Sake?"

"Sake," she squealed, "Yes, yes. I get you the best kind." She walked away, her sandals clinking on the stones.

"Boris, have a drink."

"I don't-"

"Drink on the job, I know. We aren't working right now." Matt chuckled as Boris growled once more.

"I must drive."

"Boris, one damn drink! We stay for two hours, it will be sweat out." Boris growled again.

"Why the Hell do I have such an introvert bodyguard. This town isn't unsafe, I could survive." Matt smiled wider as Boris bit the bait, cracking a small smile.

"You bust my balls a lot sir."

"Someone has to because nobody physically could." Matt felt his happiness rise in his chest. The waitress brought back a saucer and two glasses.

"Enjoy!" She smiled. The glasses sat in floating lily saucers, along with the pot. Matt poured Sake into both glasses. He pushed one across the water, the bubbles floating the glass to Boris.

"Kanpai!" Matt yelled. Boris slowly reached for his, seeing Matt's persistence. They clanked glasses and shot down the liquid. Matt gasped and laughed.

"Monda Sui!" He yelled, which meant "no worries" in Japanese. Matt poured two more shots.

"Boris," he said as he poured, "it is almost Christmas."

"I know, you keep saying that."

"Christmas is a time to reflect and gift to others, my friend. You have been a loyal associate for my two terms."

"You have been loyal to your constitutions."

"Have I?"

"The town has never been better, financially or morally."

"That is why I love our town Christmas. Give the surplus back to the people! I don't need all of that money on me, let's spend it back on them. I love our little town."

"You show that. Every day."

"Kanpai!" Matt yelled, shooting down his shot.

"I said only one."

"Then I have two!" Matt reached across the hot tub, grabbing Boris's shot and shooting it down. Boris stared at Matt sternly.

"Stop judging me. If I wanted a judge, I would call..." His threat trailed off, almost like saying his mother's name would cause her to call that moment.

"Someone needs to be by you."

"I'm a 42 year old who needs babysitting?"

"Essentially, yes."

"I hired you for protection." Matt scuffed.

"I know sir." Boris said. Matt's smile turned into a grim and curved expression as he went into thought.

"You have done well Boris."

"You are still alive, that is how I know I have done well."

"For now." Matt waved for a waitress, ignoring Boris's puzzled look.

"One more, please." Matt said. The waitress nodded and left. Matt looked back at Boris, who was still stuck with the same face.

"Do you know something I don't?"

"Me?" Matt snickered, "No."

"Sir?"

"Boris, there will be a day that you can't protect me from death."

"Not for a long time."

"Well," Matt was interrupted by the waitresses extended hands, taking the Saki as he eyed her deeply and gave a "thank you." She responded by blushing and walking away hurriedly.

"I guess we shall see."

"Sir, what do you know"

"I know," Matt took the shot," that some gifts for yourself sometimes comes with a sacrifice of others. I guess we will see what Santa brings us all on Christmas." Matt winked.

# 30 Hours before the Christmas Celebration

Mica sat in the balcony, watching her crew work around the theater diligently. She knew Klaudis was in the concession stand, preparing the drinks and food before the big day. Mike was either propping the lights or prepping his next cheesy pick up line for Klaudis. Poor guy, Mica chuckled. She remembered her awkward, less than beautiful days. Ted and Margie were managing the seats, putting blue cloths with "reserved" in gold letters over the front seats. Ted and Margie were the perfect, ideal couple. Married for fifty years in a time when you fought through the rough. Syn was on stage, dragging the podium across the stage floor as she tried to find the perfect angle where the city could easily see the dignified guest.

"Mica." A man's voice called out. Mica turned, seeing a taller, heavier set man with thinning hair. He was 28ish, but still had attractive boyish features.

"Hello Jason."

"Mica, who were those people down there?"

"Explain?"

"One had this creepy mustache. The other was about my age, tall and handsome man who was a tall glass of water and I was surprisingly thirsty in the middle of winter."

"Jason..." Mica chuckled, "they more than likely belong here."

"Mica!" A deep voice called out. Jason and Mica turned to the staircase; Dwayne was huffing up the stairs.

"Yes Dwayne?"

"For the night of, how many people are going to occupy this building?"

"Full house."

"What about the Mayor's security detail?"

"Should be just Boris and yourself."

"Great." Dwyane huffed in agitation.

"Is that a problem?"

"It just rubs me the wrong way that a politician doesn't arrive with safety nets in place."

"Well Dwyane, this town is pretty friendly when it comes down to it. I don't think we are going to have any issues."

"I don't know Mica, just rubs me the wrong way." Dwyane mumbled, walking away. Mica shook her head, trying to push her agitation aside. In her heart, nothing was going to ruin the event in two days.

# 2 Hours before the Christmas Party

Matt stood in front of his mirror, looking at his Christmas suit. He wore a red tie with a green button up undershirt. His suit jacket was black along with his dress pants and shoes.

"Looking good sir."

"Why thank you Boris. Is the car ready?"

"Yes sir."

"Great, I am going to go over my speech in the car."

"Sounds great." The two men left the house and went into black Cadillac. It was a calm, sunny day. The Sun was sinking behind the horizon, giving the city lights chance to show their beauty. The temperature was above zero, which felt like fifty degrees this time of year. Matt kept reading over his flash cards, but once the Sun was gone he started to look at the lights. Boris drove slowly through downtown so Matt could marvel at the scenery.

"Boris, I don't want to alarm you." Matt looked over at his driver, who just grunted in response.

"What does security look like tonight?"

"Tight and secure." Matt nodded absently, lost in thought.

"Have you ever thought of the weirdness of gifts?"

"Sir?"

"I mean, you stress out so bad to find the right gift. You have to find the perfect fit. Sometimes a gift to one person isn't a gift to another, you know what I mean?" Boris was slowly nodding his head.

"You are a gift to me sir. To many people."

"Again, a gift to one person may not be another." Matt tapped his fingers on the door to the beat of the music. Boris pulled up to the backstage door.

"Ready sir?" He asked, shutting the car off. He pulled out his pistol, priming it.

"Boris, not today." Matt put a hand over the pistol, making Boris huff.

"It is Christmas." Matt laughed. Both of them got out of the car, walking to the backstage door that was now opened by Dwayne.

"Are you ready sir?" Dwyane asked once Matt was at the door.

"Of course." Matt smiled.

"Ladies and gentlemen, the man you have been waiting for. Mayor Polson!" Matt passed off his jacket to Boris, heading on stage. The spotlight shined on Matt, who shook hands with the announcer and took the microphone.

"Good evening and Merry Christmas!" Matt called out. The crowd was clapping; all seats were filled with people and their beaming smiles.

"I would like to thank the Kingdom Arts Center for putting this together." Matt paced the stage, trying to look at the whole crowd.

"I am thankful to be you Mayor. I know my term is almost up, but I have had a blast with all of you. You are a wonderful group of people and we have had many victories. We have had a constant surplus, we raised our graduation and education rates, and we lowered our crime rates by making people feel like this is a home to them. We grew closer as a town and have made our small city a big impact on the state." Matt took a break for applause.

"You elected a hard working person and trusted an unique Mayor to lead this town. What were you all thinking?" Matt smiled as the crowd laughed.

"I believe my 87% approval rate from you, the people, have shown we were all happy with the outcome." Matt took another pause for the loud applause. He chuckled before he went on.

"So as my term ends, I think I owe it to you all to go to the next level." Matt paused again.

"I want your vote to be your North Dakota Congressman!" Matt cried out in excitement. The crowd went to their feet, bringing the loudest applause of the night.

"Will you follow me?" Matt yelled, the applause getting even louder and accompanied by whistles. This went on for several minutes, but then people took their seats and hung on the Mayor's every word.

"I am up front with you all because I only know one personality, the one I was born with. Let me show Congress how North Dakota will lead this country to greatness." The crowd showed their agreement with more applause.

"So enough of that talk, let's bring out the real reason we are all here." At that cue, two people from backstage wheeled a Christmas tree on a giant cart that was full of various sized presents.

"As we did last year, we will pick a piece of you seat ticket out of the mixer. Let's do present number seventeen." Mayor Polson spun the small bingo wheel, opening the door and pulled out a ticket stub.

"This present goes to seat K12!" The runner on stage grabbed the present, running down the stage steps to the crowd. Matt smiled as he saw a man stand to his feet, smiling and waving his ticket with joy. Mayor Polson lived for this moment.

Gary was leaning on the concession counter, staring deeply into Klaudis's eyes.

"I wish we were in there." Klaudis mumbled.

"I am glad we are here, together."

"Oh?" Klaudis blushed.

"Yeah, I wouldn't want to be anywhere else except here."

"I can almost sense your sarcasm."

"I'm serious." Gary smiled, Klaudis smiled as well.

"Do you like me?" Klaudis asked.

"Of course."

"No," Klaudis smiled, "you bother me all the time, you always try to be around me. Do you...Like me, like me?" Gary swallowed hard. He felt the answer stuck in his throat.

"I mean..." Gary felt his face turn red.

"Want to go help me in the basement?" Klaudis smiled.

"Refill bottles for the concession stand?" He asked innocently, which is something Gary did a lot.

"Yeah, something like that." She smiled, going around the counter to the elevator. Gary smiled, enjoying the sound of the elevator door closing behind the two.

"Let's do present number sixteen, which is for seat A16." Matt passed the package over. He froze for a moment, feeling something moving in the package.

"Sir?" The runner asked. The runner grabbed the present, running down the steps.

"Put that on the floor!" Boris screamed. The runner put the present on the ground. Boris and Dwight came from backstage, Boris covering Matt and Dwight running for the package.

"Sir, present sixteen is a toy that moves. It is a gag gift." The other runner announced.

"Sorry," Boris blushed, thoroughly embarrassed.

"Carry on." Matt laughed, the crowd laughed as well. A gunshot rang out, striking Matt in the arm. Boris pulled out his pistol. The crowd started to run to the back entrance doors frantically. Boris pointed his gun around, trying to find the assailant.

"Boris, move!" Dwight called, pulling his pistol out as well. Boris looked behind, seeing a small fire leap up the curtain. Boris ran up the stairs and grabbed Matt, pulling him off the stage. More bullets rang throughout the theater, hitting innocent people. The townsfolk pushed frantically against the doors. Boris put pressure on Matt's arm, trying to slow the bleeding. Dwyane was on his phone, calling for help.

"I told you this day would come." Matt chuckled, gritting his teeth in pain. Boris growled, pushing harder on the wound. Dwight turned just in time to take a bullet to the shoulder, making him fall back to the ground. Boris looked up, trying to locate the shooter. A female put a gun into Boris's face from his side.

"Move." She growled, Boris was too afraid to turn.

"Hello Lisa," Matt coughed, "I knew our divorce would be the death of me."

Mica and Syn were in the office common room, trying to get the workers of the Kingdom out the window to the fire escape. Jason went down the ladder, with Ted and Margie next.

"Where is Gary and Klaudis?"

"I don't know." Syn cried out, "you stay here."

"No, you stay and I'll go." Mica protested.

"Mica," Syn growled, "stay here."

Mica nodded somberly, trying to assist people out of the window. Syn took the stairs to the first floor, watching the doors bow under the pressure of the townspeople. Syn saw the thick boards holding the doors shut successfully. She pulled her pistol from a holster under her dress, loading it and moving on.

Gary and Klaudis were too busy in the dark basement to notice the commotion above. Gary knew this was illegal and Klaudis knew people would judge her for this sexual encounter, but they both enjoyed the unpractical carnal gift they were giving each other. They were on their third climax before the emergency lights and fire alarm went off. Red lights turned on in the basement, the sprinklers going off just as these two did in synch. They pulled away from each other, grabbing their clothes and trying desperately to put them on. Klaudis put her dress up and zipped it before Gary even had his pants on. Gary heard footsteps coming down the stairs. Gary looked down the hallway which was basked in red lights, his fear creeping into his chest as he saw a man bathed in the red light and staring back at him.

"Gary." Klaudis whispered, grabbing him tightly, "get dressed." Gary felt that grip was his courage, running down the hall with no shoes or shirt. Gary yelled as he ran, a flash of light went into the hall. He ran into the man, straddling him to the ground and hammer punching him in the face multiple times. It was then he could hear the flame crackling from the staircase above. Gary missed with his next punch, too distracted about smelling the smoke, and cracked his knuckles painfully on the concrete.

"Gary!" Klaudis cried out. He turned, trying to find her in the red light. Gary sent an elbow to the assailant, hearing a crunch of bone. He went to his feet, grabbing the man by his shirt and dragging him easily down the hall. He had a hard time gripping him, but adrenaline took over. Gary saw the outline of Klaudis, shirt and shoes in hand. He quickly put his shirt on and threw his shoes on as well, not taking time to tie the laces. Gary and Klaudis dragged the man upstairs. Once they reached the first floor, they dropped the man so they could inspect him better.

"Gary, look." Klaudis pointed to the barred doors.

"What the hell?" Gary whispered, feeling the questions prick at his senses. Something bad was going on, he could feel it. Gary looked forward, but quickly turned as Klaudis cried out in fear. Gary turned to encounter a new assailant.

"Syn!" Gary yelled. Syn had Klaudis around her neck, gun pointed at Gary.

"I'm sorry Gary. Money kills." She fired next to Klaudis's ear, making her cry out in pain. Gary collapsed to the wall, looking at not one hole in his chest, but two. Gary understood why he couldn't grip the man as he looked down his arm and saw blood pooling from his hand. Klaudis went the ground, holding her ears in pain. Syn went to escape, turning around, but was confronted with the doors busting open and the crowd running through. She couldn't make her way through the wave of people. She cursed, hoping the plans were still in effect.

"Goodbye Boris." Matt's ex-wife laughed. She pulled the trigger; the gun kicked and caught Boris just on top of his shoulder. She looked up to the stage, which was now fully engulfed in flames. She took one ore look at Matt, who was breathing slowly.

"I killed you because I don't understand why everyone loved you, except me." She pointed her gun at Matt, pulling back the hammer of the gun.

"You ruined my name. I can't go anywhere without people calling me the 'Mayor's Ex.' I have a name, and now the town will know I am so much more important than you. I don't want to see your face anymore in this town, besides a piece in the obituary section stating your pathetic life."

She shot him in the other arm, putting the pistol away and following the crowd that was now rushing out of the theater. She felt in the clear, until someone tackled her to the ground. She tried to pull out her gun again, but Dwayne was quick to disarm her.

"You are under arrest." Dwayne stood to his feet, pulling the flailing body of Matt's ex-wife with him. They fought through the crowd, making their way into the main area. Dwayne didn't even notice the cries of pain from Gary and Klaudis as the crowd pushed him outside. Once outside, he found Mica trying to herd the people away from the building.

"Don't let her out of your sights." Dwayne ordered. Mica nodded, pulling her off Dwayne's shoulder and directing her to the cops waiting outside. Dwayne pushed through the crowd, looking for any stragglers. He heard the cries for help, following them until he found Gary leaning against the concession table. Gary pointed to a man who was lying face down, just aside from the horde of people. Dwayne went to the man, pulling him by the arms and onto his shoulders. Klaudis tried to crawl to Dwayne. Dwayne easily scooped her little frame up and started to help her to the door. Gary went on the other side of Dwayne, using him as a crutch and crying out as the blood drenched his pants.

"Syn, did this." Gary coughed before he screamed again, "the man on your shoulder tried to kill us in the basement."

"Let's worry about them later, let's get out of here." Dwayne said as they finally made their way outside.

The Kingdom Arts crew gathered together outside, the townsfolk also observing from a distance as the theater for the lonely people burnt a scar into all of their lives. Mica, finally given a moment, cried as she watched her hard work and dreams burnt to the ground. She cried as she lost two homes in the same week. The elderly couple stood beside her, trying to consul her. Jason was beside her, trying as well. EMT'S tended to the dead and dying, Gary watched with dead eyes as Klaudis was wheeled into the ambulance. Klaudis watched as a sheet was put over Gary and he was wheeled away. Klaudis also watched as a lone woman walked through the alleyway, escaping the scene before anyone could catch what she had done. That was the last time anyone had seen or heard from Syn again, as she had a ticket back to Russia waiting for her. To Russia, where they would protect her. Boris was the last one out of the Empire, holding his dead friend, his dead boss, the dead Mayor. Dwayne was tended to after he helped hand the ex-wife over to the police. Little did the sleepy town know what happened, but the ex-wife helped fill in the blanks by selling out her accomplices and motives for a couple of years off from her sentence. Syn wished for the demise of Mica, who always seemed to be better than her. Mica tried to keep her and the rest of the crew busy upstairs. Syn was paid to help by the mustache man seen helping the crew prepare a couple of days ago, only he was preparing to burn the stage down by placing gas cans below. Michel Brady, the loser of the Mayor race, the brains and money of the mission. Micheal was the man who barred the doors of the people who didn't vote for him, once Gary and Klaudis went downstairs of course, and quickly ran through the basement hall to set fire to the curtains. With the money of Michael, the jealousy of Syn, and the hatred of a great man by Lisa, everybody of the town was left in the cold on that fateful Christmas day, without a place for the lonely people to gather forevermore.